SWEEP #4

Dark Magick

Cate Tiernan

PUFFIN BOOKS

Dark Magick

Puffin Books
Published by the Penguin Group
Penguin Putnam Books for Young Readers,
345 Hudson Street, New York, New York 10014, U.S.A.
Penguin Books Ltd, 27 Wrights Lane, London W8 5TZ, England
Penguin Books Australia Ltd, Ringwood, Victoria, Australia
Penguin Books Canada Ltd, 10 Alcorn Avenue, Toronto, Ontario, Canada M4V 3B2
Penguin Books (N.Z.) Ltd, 182-190 Wairau Road, Auckland 10, New Zealand

Penguin Books Ltd, Registered Offices: Harmondsworth, Middlesex, England

Published by Puffin Books,
a division of Penguin Putnam Books for Young Readers, 2001

1 3 5 7 9 10 8 6 4 2

 Produced by 17th Street Productions,
an Alloy Online, Inc. company
33 West 17th Street
New York, NY 10011

17th Street Productions and associated logos
are trademarks and/or registered trademarks of Alloy Online, Inc.

ISBN 0-14-131112-6

Printed in the United States of America

For my mùirn beatha dàn

1.
Falling

November 1999

The council pronounced me not guilty of killing Linden. The vote of the seven elders of the Great Clans was not unanimous, though. The Vikroth representative and the Wyndenkell, my mother's own clanswoman, voted against me.

I had almost hoped they would condemn me, for then at least my life's path would be certain. And in a way, I was guilty, was I not? I filled Linden's head with my talk of vengeance, and opened his mind to the idea of calling on the darkness. If I had not actually killed my brother, then I knew he had found his way to his death along a path I had shown him.

When I was found innocent, I felt lost. I knew only that I would spend the rest of my life atoning for Linden's death.

—Giomanach

Snowflakes mixed with sleet whipped at my cheeks. I stumbled through the snow, supporting my boyfriend Cal's weight against me, my feet growing leaden and icy in my clogs. Cal stumbled, and I braced myself. In the moonlight I peered up at his face, alarmed by how white he looked, how beaten, how ill. I trudged through the dark woods, feeling like every step away from the cliff took an hour.

The cliff. In my mind, I saw Hunter Niall falling backward, his arms windmilling as he went over the edge. Bile rose in my throat, and I swallowed convulsively. Yes, Cal was a mess, but Hunter was probably dead. Dead! And Cal and I had killed him. I drew in a shuddering breath as Cal swayed against me.

Together we stumbled through the woods, accompanied only by the malevolent hiss of the sleet in the black branches around us. Where was Cal's house?

"Are we headed the right way?" I asked Cal. The freezing wind snatched the words from my throat.

Cal blinked. One eye was swollen shut and already purple. His beautiful mouth was bloody, and his lower lip was split.

"Never mind," I said, looking ahead. "I think this is it."

By the time Cal's house was in view, we were both soaked through and frozen. Anxiously I scanned the circular driveway for Selene Belltower's car, but Cal's mother was still out. Not good. I needed help.

"Tired," Cal said fuzzily as I helped him up the steps. Somehow we made it through the front door, but once inside, there was no way I could get him up to his attic room.

"There." Cal gestured with a hand swollen from punching Hunter. Feeling unbearably weary, I lurched through the parlor doors and helped Cal collapse on the blue sofa. He toppled over, curling to fit on the cushions. He was shaking with cold, his face shocked and pale.

"Cal," I said, "we need to call 911. About Hunter. Maybe they can find him. It might not be too late."

Cal's face crinkled in a grotesque approximation of a laugh. His split lip oozed blood, and his cheek was mottled with angry bruises. "It's too late," he croaked, his teeth chattering. "I'm positive." He nodded toward the fireplace, his eyes shut. "Fire."

Was it too late for Hunter? A tiny part of me almost hoped it was—if Hunter was dead, then we couldn't help him, and I didn't even have to try.

But was he? A sob rose in my throat. Was he?

Okay, I thought, trying to calm down. Okay. Break down the situation. Make a plan. I knelt and clumsily piled newspaper and kindling on the grate. I chose three large logs and arranged them on top.

I didn't see any matches, so, closing my eyes, I tried to summon fire with my mind. But my magickal powers felt almost nonexistent. In fact, just trying to call on them made my head ache sharply. After nearly seventeen years of living without magick, to find myself bereft of it now was terrifying. I opened my eyes and looked wildly around. Finally I saw an Aim 'n' Flame on the mantel, and I grabbed it and popped its trigger.

The paper and kindling caught. I swayed toward the flames, feeling their healing warmth, then I glanced at Cal again. He looked wretched.

"Cal?" I helped him sit up enough to tug him out of his leather jacket, taking care not to scrape his wrists, which were raw and blistered where Hunter had tried to bind them with a strange magickal chain. I pulled off Cal's wet boots. Then I covered him up with a patchwork velvet throw that was draped artistically over one end of the couch. He squeezed my fingers and tried to smile at me.

"Be right back," I said, and hurried to the kitchen. I felt horribly alone as I waited for water to boil. I ran upstairs and rummaged through the first bathroom I found for bandages, then went back down and fixed a pot of herb tea. A pale face with accusing green eyes seemed to form in the steam that rose from the top of the teapot. Hunter, oh, God, Hunter.

Hunter had tried to kill Cal, I reminded myself. He might have tried to kill me, too. Still, it was Hunter who had gone over the edge of the cliff into the Hudson River, the river filled with ice chunks as big as his head. It was Hunter who had probably been swept away by the current and Hunter whose body would be found tomorrow. Or not. I clamped my lips together to keep from sobbing as I hurried back to Cal.

Slowly I got Cal to drink a whole mug of goldenseal-and-ginger tea. His color looked better when he had finished it. I gently swabbed his wrists with a damp cloth, then wrapped them with a roll of gauze I had found, but the skin was blistered, and I knew it must hurt incredibly.

After the tea Cal lay down again and slept, his breathing uneven. Should I have given him Tylenol? Should I hunt around for witch-type medicine? In the short while I had known Cal, he had been the strong one in our relationship. I had counted on him. Now he was counting on me, and I didn't know if I was ready.

The mantel clock above my head struck three slow chimes. I stared at it. Three o'clock in the morning! I set my mug down on the coffee table. I was supposed to be home by one. And I didn't even have my car—Cal had picked me up. He was clearly in no shape to drive. Selene wasn't back yet. Dammit! I said to myself. Think, think.

I could call my dad and have him come get me. Very unappealing option.

It was too late to call the only taxi service in Widow's Vale, which was in essence Ed Jinkins in his old Cutlass Supreme hanging out at the commuter station.

I could take Cal's car.

Five minutes later I let myself out of the house carefully. Cal was still asleep. I had taken the keys from his jacket, then written a note of explanation and tucked it in his jeans pocket, hoping he would understand. I stopped dead when I saw Hunter's gray sedan sitting in the driveway like an accusation. Crap! What to do about his car?

There was nothing I could do. Hunter had the keys. And he was gone. I couldn't push the car anywhere by myself and anyway, that seemed so—methodical somehow. So planned.

My head spun. What should I do? Waves of exhaustion flowed over me, almost making me weep. But I had to accept the fact that I couldn't do anything about this. Cal or Selene would have to deal with Hunter's car. Trembling, I climbed into Cal's gold Explorer, turned on the brights, and headed for home.

Cal had used spells on me tonight, spells of binding so I couldn't move. Why? So I wouldn't interfere in his battle with Hunter? So I wouldn't be hurt? Or because he didn't trust me? Well, if he hadn't trusted me before, he knew better now. I clamped my teeth together on a semihysterical giggle. It wasn't every girl who would throw a Wiccan ceremonial dagger into the neck of her boyfriend's enemy.

Hunter had tried to kill Cal, had bound his hands with spelled silver chain that had started to sizzle against Cal's flesh as soon as it touched him. That was when I'd hurled the athame at him and sent him over the cliff's edge. And probably killed him. Killed him.

I shuddered as I turned onto my street. *Had* we actually killed him? Did Hunter have a chance? Maybe the wound in his neck wasn't as horrific as it had seemed. Maybe, when he went over the cliff, he had landed on a ledge. Maybe he was found by a park ranger or someone like that.

Maybe.

I let the Explorer drift to a halt around the corner from my house. As I pocketed the keys, I noticed all the birthday gifts Cal had given me earlier, piled up on the backseat. Well, almost all. The beautiful athame was gone—Hunter had taken it over the cliff with him. With a sense of unreality I gathered up the other gifts and then ran home down the shoveled and salted walks. I let myself in silently, feeling with my senses. Again my magick was like a single match being held in a storm wind instead of the powerful wave I was used to feeling. I couldn't detect much of anything.

To my relief, my parents didn't stir as I went past their bedroom door. In my own room I sat for a moment on the edge of my bed, collecting my strength. After the nightmarish events of tonight my bedroom looked babyish, as if it belonged to a stranger. The pink-and-white-striped walls, flowered border, and frilly curtains had never been me, anyway. Mom had picked everything out and redone the room for me as a surprise while I was at camp, six years ago.

I threw off my clammy clothes and sighed with relief as I pulled on sweats. Then I went downstairs and dialed 911.

"What is the nature of the emergency?" a crisp voice asked.

"I saw someone fall into the Hudson," I said quickly, speaking through a tissue like they did in old movies. "About two miles up from the North Bridge." This was an estimate, based on where I thought Cal's house was. "Someone fell in. He may need help." I hung up quickly, hoping I hadn't stayed on the phone long enough for the call to be traced. How did that work? Did I have to stay on for a minute? Thirty seconds? Oh, Jesus. If they tracked me down I would confess everything. I couldn't live with this burden on my soul.

My mind was racing with everything that had happened: my wonderful, romantic birthday with Cal; almost making love but then backing out; all my gifts; the magick we shared; my birth mother's athame, which I had shown Cal tonight and was now clutching like a security blanket; then the battle with Hunter, the horror as he fell. And now it was too late, Cal said. But was it? I had to try one last thing.

I put on my wet coat, went outside, and walked around the side of my house in the darkness. Holding my birth mother's athame, I leaned close to a windowsill. There, glowing faintly beneath the knife's power, shimmered a sigil. Sky Eventide and Hunter had surrounded my house with the charms; I still didn't know why. But I hoped this would work.

Once more closing my eyes, I held the athame over the

sigil. I concentrated, feeling like I was about to pass out. Sky, I thought, swallowing. Sky.

I hated Sky Eventide. Everything about her filled me with loathing and distrust, just as Hunter did, though for some reason Hunter upset me more. But she was his ally, and she was the person who should be told about him. I sent my thought out toward the purplish snow clouds. Sky. Hunter is in the river, by Cal's house. Go get him. He needs your help.

What am I doing? I thought, beyond weariness. I can't even light a match. I can't feel my family sleeping inside my house. My magick is gone. But still I stood there in the cold darkness, my eyes closed, my hand turning to a frozen claw around the knife handle. Hunter is in the river. Go get him. Go get Hunter. Hunter is in the river.

Tears came without warning, shockingly warm against my chilled cheeks. Gasping, I stumbled back inside and hung up my coat. Then I slowly mounted the steps, one by one, and was dimly surprised when I made it to the top. I hid my mother's athame under my mattress and crawled into bed. My kitten, Dagda, stretched sleepily, then moved up to coil himself next to my neck. I curled one hand around him. Huddled under my comforter, I shook with cold and wept until the first blades of sunlight pierced the childish, ruffled curtains at my window.

2.
Guilty

November 1999

Uncle Beck, Aunt Shelagh, and Cousin Athan held a small celebration for me back at the house, after the trial. But my heart was full of pain.

I sat at the kitchen table. Aunt Shelagh and Alwyn were swooping around, arranging food on plates. Then Uncle Beck came in. He told me that I'd been cleared of the blame and I must let it go.

"How can I?" I asked. It was I who'd first tried to use dark magick to find our parents. Though Linden had acted alone in calling on the dark spectre that killed him, he wouldn't have had the idea if I hadn't put it into his head.

Then Alwyn spoke up. She said I was wrong, that Linden had always liked the dark side. She said he liked the power, and that he'd thought making herb mixtures was beneath him.

Her halo of corkscrew curls, fiery red like our Mum's, seemed to quiver as she spoke.

"What are you on about?" I asked her. "Linden never mentioned any of this to me."

She said Linden had believed I wouldn't understand. He'd told her he wanted to be the most powerful witch anyone had ever seen. Her words were like needles in my heart.

Uncle Beck asked why she hadn't told us sooner, and she said she had. I saw her jut her chin in that obstinate way she has. And Aunt Shelagh thought about it, and said, "You know, she did. She did tell me. I thought she was telling stories."

Alwyn said no one had believed her because she was just a kid. Then she left the room, while Uncle Beck, Aunt Shelagh, and I sat in the kitchen and weighed our guilt.

—Giomanach

I woke up on my seventeenth birthday feeling like someone had put me in a blender and set it to chop. Sleepily I blinked and checked my clock. Nine. Dawn had come at six, so I had gotten a big three hours' sleep. Great. And then I thought—is Hunter dead? Did I kill him? My stomach roiled, and I wanted to cry.

Under the covers, I felt a small warm body creeping cautiously along my side. When Dagda poked his little gray head out from under the covers, I stroked his ears.

"Hi, little guy," I said softly. I sat up just as the door to my room opened.

"Morning, birthday girl!" my mom said brightly. She crossed my room and pushed aside the curtains, filling my room with brittle sunlight.

"Morning," I said, trying to sound normal. A vision of my mom finding out about Hunter made me shudder. It would destroy her.

She sat on my bed and kissed my forehead, as if I was seven instead of seventeen. Then she peered at me. "Do you feel all right?" She pressed the back of her hand against my forehead. "Hmmm. No fever. But your eyes look a bit red and puffy."

"I'm okay. Just tired," I mumbled. Time to change the subject. I had a sudden thought. "Is today really my actual birthday?" I asked.

Mom stroked my hair back from my face with a gentle hand. "Of course it is. Morgan, you've seen your birth certificate," she reminded me.

"Oh, right." Until a few weeks ago I had always believed I was a Rowlands, like the rest of my family. But when I met Cal and began exploring Wicca, it became clear that I had magickal powers and that I was a blood witch, from a long line of blood witches—witches from one of the Seven Great Clans of Wicca. That's how I'd found out I was adopted. Since then it had been pretty much of an emotional roller-coaster ride here at home. But I loved my parents, Sean and Mary Grace Rowlands, and my sister, Mary K., who was their biological daughter. And they loved me. And they were trying to come to terms with my Wiccan heritage, my legacy. As was I.

"Now, since today is your birthday, you can do what you

want, more or less," Mom said, absently tickling Dagda's bat-like gray ears. "Do you want to have a big breakfast and we'll go to a later mass? Or we can go to church now and then do something special for lunch?"

I don't want to go to church at all, I thought. Lately my relationship with church had seemed like a battle of wills as I struggled to integrate Wicca into my life. I also couldn't face the idea of sitting through a Catholic mass and then having lunch with my family after what had happened the night before. "Um, is it all right if I just sleep in today?" I asked. "I am feeling a little under the weather, actually. You guys do church and lunch without me."

Mom's lips thinned, but after a moment she nodded. "All right," she said. "If that's what you want." She stood up. "Do you want us to bring you back something for lunch?"

The idea of food repulsed me. "Oh, no thanks," I said, trying to sound casual. "I'll just find something in the fridge. Thanks, anyway, though."

"Okay," Mom said, touching my forehead again. "Tonight Eileen and Paula are coming over, and we'll do dinner and cake and presents. Sound good?"

"Great," I said, and Mom closed the door behind her. I sank back on my pillow. I felt as if I had a split personality. On the one hand, I was Morgan Rowlands, good daughter, honor roll student, math whiz, observant Catholic. On the other hand, I was a witch, by heritage and inclination.

I stretched, feeling the ache in my muscles. The events of the night before hovered over my head like a storm cloud. What had I done? How had I come to this? If only I knew for sure whether or not Hunter was dead. . . .

I waited until I heard the front door close behind my family. Then I got up and began pulling on my clothes. I knew what I had to do next.

I drove my car to the back road that ran behind Cal's house and parked. Then I crunched across the snow to the cliff's rocky edge. Carefully I stretched out on my stomach and peered over. If I saw Hunter's body, I would have to climb down there, I warned myself. If he was alive, I would go for help. If he was dead . . . I wasn't sure what I would do.

Later I would go up to Cal's house and see how he was, but first I needed to do this, to look for Hunter. Had Sky gotten my message? Had 911 responded?

The ground around this area was churned and muddy, evidence of the horrific battle Hunter and Cal had fought. It was awful to think about it, to remember how helpless I had been under Cal's binding spell. Why had he done that to me?

I leaned over farther to try to see beneath a rocky ledge. The icy Hudson swept beneath me, clean and deadly. Sharp rocks jutted up from the riverbed. If Hunter had hit them, if he'd been in the water any length of time, he was surely dead. The thought made my stomach clench up again. In my mind I pictured Hunter falling in slow motion over the edge, his neck streaming blood, an expression of surprise on his face. . . .

"Looking for something?"

I turned quickly, already scrambling to my feet as I recognized the English-accented voice. Sky Eventide.

She stood fifteen feet away, hands in her pockets. Her

pale face, whitish blond hair, and black eyes seemed etched against the painful blue of the sky.

"What are you doing here?" I said.

"I was about to ask the same thing," she said, stepping toward me. She was taller than me and as thin. Her black leather jacket didn't look warm enough for the cold.

I said nothing, and she went on, a razor's edge in her voice. "Hunter didn't come home last night. I felt his presence here. But now I don't feel it at all."

She hasn't found Hunter. Hunter's dead. Oh, Goddess, I thought.

"What happened here?" she went on, her face like stone in the cold, bright sun. "The ground looks like it was plowed. There's blood everywhere." She stepped closer to me, fierce and cold, like a Viking. "Tell me what you know about it."

"I don't know anything," I said, too loudly. *Hunter's dead.*

"You're lying. You're a lying Woodbane, just like Cal and Selene," Sky said bitterly, spitting out the words as if she were saying, You're filth, you're garbage.

The world shifted around me, became slightly unreal. There was snow beneath my feet, water below the cliff, trees behind Sky, but it was like a stage set.

"Cal and Selene aren't Woodbane," I said. My mouth was dry.

Sky tossed her head. "Of course they are," she said. "And you're just like them. You'll stop at nothing to keep your power."

"That's not true," I snapped.

"Last night Hunter was on his way to Cal's place, on council business. He was going to confront Cal. I think you were there, too, since you're Cal's little lapdog. Now tell me what happened." Her voice rang out like steel, actually hurting my ears, and I felt the strength of her personality pressing on me. I wanted to spill out everything I knew. All of a sudden I realized she was putting a spell on me. A flash of rage seared through me. How dare she?

I straightened up and deliberately walled off my mind.

Sky's eyes flickered. "You don't know what you're doing," she said, her words chipping away at me. "That makes you dangerous. I'll be watching you. And so will the council."

She whirled and disappeared into the woods, her short, sunlight-colored hair riffling in the breeze.

The woods were silent after she left. No birds chirped, no leaves stirred, the wind itself died. After several minutes I went back to my car and drove it up to Cal's house. Hunter's car was no longer there. I climbed the stone steps and rang the doorbell, feeling a fresh wash of fear as I wondered what I might find, what might have happened to Cal since I left.

Selene opened the door. She was wearing an apron, and the faint scent of herbs clung to her. There was a wealth of warmth and concern in her golden eyes as she reached out and hugged me to her. She had never hugged me before, and I closed my eyes, enjoying the lovely feeling of comfort and relief she offered.

Then Selene withdrew and looked deeply into my face. "I heard about last night. Morgan, you saved my son's life," she said, her voice low and melodious. "Thank you." She looped her arm through mine and drew me inside, shutting out the rest of the world. We walked down the hallway to the large, sunny kitchen at the back of the house.

"How is Cal?" I managed.

"He's better," she said. "Thanks to you. I came home and found him in the parlor, and he managed to tell me most of what happened. I've been doing some healing work with him."

"I didn't know what to do," I said helplessly. "He fell asleep, and I had to get home. I have his car at my house," I added inanely.

Selene nodded. "We'll come get it later," she said, and I dug in my pocket and gave her the keys. She took them and pushed open the kitchen door.

I sniffed the air. "What's that?" I asked.

Now I noticed that the kitchen was ablaze with light, sound, color, scent. I paused in the doorway, trying to separate out the different stimuli. Selene walked over to the stove to stir something, and I realized she had a small, three-legged cast-iron cauldron bubbling on the burner of her range. The odd thing was how normal it looked somehow.

She caught my glance and said, "Usually I do all this outside. But this autumn has been so awful, weatherwise." She stirred slowly with a long wooden spoon, then leaned over and inhaled, the steam making her face flush slightly.

"What are you making?" I asked, moving closer.

"This is a vision potion," she explained. "When ingested by a knowledgeable witch, it aids with scrying and divination."

"Like a hallucinogen?" I asked, a little shocked. Images of LSD and mushrooms and people freaking out flashed through my mind.

Selene laughed. "No. It's just an aid, to make it easier to find your visions. I only make it every four or five years or so. I don't use it that often, and a little goes a long way."

On the gleaming granite counter I saw labeled vials and small jars and, at one end, a stack of homemade candles.

"Did you do all this?" I asked.

Selene nodded and brushed her dark hair away from her face. "I always go through a flurry of activity around this time of year. Samhain is over, Yule hasn't begun—I suppose I just itch for something to do. Years ago I started making many of my own tinctures and essential oils and infusions—they're always fresher and better than what you can buy in the store. Have you ever made candles?"

"No."

Selene looked around the kitchen, at the bustle and clutter, and said, "Things you make, cook, sew, decorate—those are all expressions of the power and homages to the Goddess." Busily she stirred the cauldron, deasil, and then tasted a tiny bit on the end of her spoon.

At any other time I would have found this impromptu lesson fascinating, but at the moment I was too keyed up to focus on it. "Will Cal be okay?" I blurted out.

"Yes," Selene said. She looked directly at me. "Do you want to talk about Hunter?"

That was all it took, and suddenly I was crying silently, my shoulders shaking, my face burning. In a moment she was beside me, holding me. A tissue appeared, and I took it.

"Selene," I said shakily, "I think he's dead."

"Shhh," she said soothingly. "Poor darling. Sit down. Let me give you some tea."

Tea? I thought wildly. I think I *killed* someone, and you're offering me *tea*?

But it was witch tea, and within seconds of my first sip I felt my emotions calm slightly, enough to get myself under control. Selene sat across the table from me, looking into my eyes.

"Hunter tried to kill Cal," she said intently. "He might have tried to kill you, too. Anyone standing there would have done what you did. You saw a friend in danger, and you acted. No one could blame you for that."

"I didn't mean to hurt Hunter," I said, my voice wavering.

"Of course you didn't," she agreed. "You just wanted to stop him. There was no way to predict what would happen. Listen to me, my dear. If you hadn't done what you did, if you hadn't been so quick thinking and loyal, then it would be Cal now in the river, and I would be mourning him and possibly you, too. Hunter came here looking for trouble. He was on our property. He was out for blood. You and Cal both acted in self-defense."

Slowly I drank my tea. The way Selene put it, it sounded reasonable, even inevitable. "Do you—do you think we should go to the police?" I asked.

Selene cocked her head to one side, considering. "No," she said after a moment. "The difficulty is that there were no other witnesses. And that knife wound in Hunter's neck would be hard to explain as self-defense, even though you and I both know that's the truth of it."

A fresh wave of dread washed over me. She was right. To the police, it would probably look like murder.

I remembered something else. "And his car," I said. "Did you move it?"

Selene nodded. "I spelled it to start and drove it to an

abandoned barn just outside of town. It sounds premeditated, I know, but it seemed the prudent thing to do." She reached out and covered my hand with her own. "I know it's hard. I know you feel that your life will never be the same. But you must try to let it go, my dear."

I swallowed miserably. "I feel so guilty," I said.

"Let me tell you about Hunter," she said, and her voice was suddenly almost harsh. I shivered.

"I've heard reports about him," Selene went on. "By all accounts he was a loose cannon, someone who could not be trusted. Even the council had their doubts about him, thought he had gone too far, too many times. He's been obsessed with Woodbanes all his life, and in the last few years this obsession had taken a deadly turn." She seemed quite serious, and I nodded.

A thought occurred to me. "Then why was he going after Cal?" I asked. "You guys don't know what clan you are, right? I heard Hunter call Cal Woodbane—did he think Cal . . . wait—" I shook my head, confused. Cal had told me that he and Hunter probably had the same father. And Sky had said Cal was Woodbane like his father. Which made both Cal and Hunter half Woodbane? I couldn't keep all this straight.

"Who knows what he thought?" said Selene. "He was clearly crazy. I mean, this is someone who killed his own brother."

My eyebrows knitted. I vaguely remembered Cal throwing that accusation at Hunter last night. "What do you mean?"

Selene shook her head, then started as her cauldron

hissed and spat on the stove, almost boiling over. She hurried over to adjust the flame. For the next few minutes she was very busy, and I hesitated to interrupt her.

"Do you think I could see Cal?" I asked finally.

She looked back at me regretfully. "I'm sorry, Morgan, but I gave him a drink to make him sleep. He probably won't wake up until tonight."

"Oh." I stood up and retrieved my coat, unwilling to pursue the story about Hunter if Selene didn't want to tell me. I felt a thousand times better than I had, but I knew instinctively the pain and guilt would return.

"Thank you for coming," Selene said, straining a steaming mixture over the sink. "And remember, what you did last night was the right thing. Believe that."

I nodded awkwardly.

"Please call me if you want to talk," Selene added as I headed for the door. "Anytime."

"Thank you," I said. I pushed through the door and headed home.

3.
Dread

April 2000

Scrying doesn't always mean you see a picture—it can be more like receiving impressions. I use my lueg, my scrying stone. It's a big, thick chunk of obsidian, almost four inches at its widest and tapering to a point. It was my father's. I found it under my pillow the morning he and Mum disappeared.

Luegs are more reliable than either fire or water. Fire may show you pasts and possible futures, but it's hard to work with. There's an old Wiccan saying that goes: Fire is a fragile lover, court her well, neglect her not; her faith is like a misty smoke, her anger is destructive hot. Water is easier to use but very misleading. Once I heard Mum say that water is the Wiccan whore, spilling her secrets to any, lying to most, trusting few.

Last night I took my lueg and went down to the kill that flows at the edge of my uncle's property. This was where we swam in the summer, where Linden and I caught minnows, where Alwyn used to pick gooseberries.

I sat at the water's edge and scryed, looking deep into my obsidian, weaving spells of vision.

After a long, long time, the rock's face cleared, and in its depths I saw my mother. It was my mother of all those years ago, right before she disappeared. I remember the day clearly. An eight-year-old me ran up to where she knelt in the garden, pulling weeds. She looked up, saw me, and her face lit, as if I was the sun. Giomanach, she said, and looked at me with love, the sunlight glinting off her bright hair. Seeing her in the lueg, I was almost crushed with longing and a childish need to see her, have her hold me.

When the stone went blank, I held it in my hand, then crumpled over and cried on the bank of the kill.

—Giomanach

My birthday dinner was like a movie. I felt like I was watching myself through a window, smiling, talking to people, opening presents. I was glad to see Aunt Eileen and her girlfriend, Paula Steen, again—and Mom and Mary K. had worked hard to make everything special. It would have been a great birthday, except for the horrific images that kept crashing into my brain. Hunter and Cal grappling in the churned, bloody snow. Myself, sinking to my knees under Cal's binding spell, then me looking down at the athame in my hand and looking up to see Hunter. Hunter, rivulets of blood on his neck, going over the edge of the cliff.

"Hey, are you all right?" Mary K. asked me as I stood by the window, gazing out into the darkness. "You seem kind of out of it."

"Just tired," I told her. I added quickly, "But I'm having a great time. Thanks, Mary K."

"We aim to please." She flashed me a grin.

Finally Aunt Eileen and Paula left, and I went upstairs and called Cal. His voice sounded weak and scratchy.

"I'm okay," he said. "Are you okay?"

"Yes," I said. "Physically."

"I know." He sighed. "I can't believe it. I didn't mean for him to go over the edge. I just wanted to stop him." He laughed dryly, a croaking sound. "Helluva seventeenth birthday. I'm sorry, Morgan."

"It wasn't your fault," I said. "He came after you."

"I didn't want him to hurt you."

"But why did you put binding spells on me?" I asked.

"I was afraid. I didn't want you to jump into the middle of it and get hurt," Cal said.

"I wanted to help you. I hated being frozen like that. It was awful."

"I'm so sorry, Morgan," Cal breathed. "Everything was happening so fast, and I thought I was acting for the best."

"Don't ever do that to me again."

"I won't, I promise. I'm sorry."

"Okay. I called 911 when I got home," I admitted softly. "And I sent Sky an anonymous witch message, telling her where to look for Hunter."

Cal was silent for a minute. Then he said, "You did the right thing. I'm glad you did."

"It didn't help, though. I saw Sky at the river this morning. She said Hunter didn't come home last night. She was sure I knew something about it."

"What did you tell her?"

"That I didn't know what she was talking about. She said she didn't feel Hunter's presence or something like that. And she called me a lying Woodbane."

"That bitch," Cal said angrily.

"Could she find out about what happened somehow? Using magick?"

"No," said Cal. "My mom put warding spells around the whole place to block anyone from scrying and seeing what happened. Don't worry."

"I am worried," I insisted. A bubble of panic was rising in my throat again. "This is horrible. I can't stand it."

"Morgan! Try to calm down," said Cal. "It will all be okay, you'll see. I won't let anything happen to you. The only thing is, I'm afraid Sky is going to be a problem. Hunter was her cousin, and she's not going to let this rest. Tomorrow we'll spell your house and your car with wards of protection. But still—be on your guard."

"Okay." Dread settled more heavily on my shoulders as I hung up. Wherever this is going, I thought, there's no way it can end well. No way at all.

On Monday morning I got up early and grabbed the morning paper before anyone else could see it. Widow's Vale doesn't have its own daily paper, just a twice-monthly publication that's mostly pickup articles from other papers. I quickly paged through the *Albany Times Union* to see if there was any mention of a body being fished out of the Hudson. There wasn't. I gnawed my lip. What did that mean? Had his body not been found yet? Or was it just that we weren't close enough to Albany for them to cover the story?

I drove with Mary K. to school and parked outside the building, feeling like I had aged five years over the weekend.

As I turned off the engine, Bakker Blackburn, Mary K.'s boyfriend, trotted up to meet her. "Hey, babe," he said, nuzzling her neck.

Mary K. giggled and pushed him away. He took her book bag from her, and they went off to meet their friends.

Robbie Gurevitch, one of my best friends and a member of my coven, strolled up to my car. A group of freshman girls stared admiringly at him as he passed them, and I saw him blush. Being gorgeous was new to him—until I'd given him a healing potion a month ago, he'd had horrible acne. But the potion had cleared up his skin and even erased the scars.

"Are you going to fix your car?" he asked me.

I looked at my broken headlight and smashed nose and sighed. A few days ago I'd thought someone was following me, and I had skidded on a patch of ice and crunched my beloved behemoth of a car, fondly known as Das Boot, into a ditch. At the time it had seemed utterly terrifying, but since the events of Saturday night, it felt more in perspective.

"Yep," I said, scanning the area for Cal. That morning I'd noticed the Explorer was gone from my block, but I didn't know if he'd be back at school today.

"I'm guessing it'll cost at least five hundred bucks," Robbie said.

We walked toward the old, redbrick former courthouse that was now Widow's Vale High. I was striving for normalcy, trying to be old reliable Morgan. "I wanted to ask you—did you go to Bree's coven's circle on Saturday?" Bree Warren had been my other best friend since childhood— my closest friend—until we fought over Cal. Now she hated me. And I . . . I didn't know what I felt about her. I was furious at her. I didn't trust her. I missed her fiercely.

"I did go." Robbie held the door open for me. "It was small and kind of lame. But that English witch, Sky Eventide, the one who leads their circles . . ." He whistled. "She had power coming off her in waves."

"I know Sky," I said stiffly. "I met her at Cal's. What did you guys do? Did Sky mention me or Cal?"

He looked at me. "No. We just did a circle. It was interesting because Sky does it slightly differently than Cal. Why would she mention you or Cal?"

"Different how?" I pressed, ignoring his question. "You guys didn't, um, do anything scary, did you? Like call on spirits or anything?"

Robbie stopped walking. "No. It was just a circle, Morgan. I think we can safely say that Bree and Raven are not having their souls sucked out by the devil."

I gave him an exasperated look. "Wiccans don't believe in the devil," I reminded him. "I just want to make sure that Bree isn't getting into anything dangerous or bad." *Like I did.*

We walked to the basement stairs, where our coven, Cirrus, usually hung out in the morning. Ethan Sharp was already there, doing his English homework. Jenna Ruiz sat across from him, reading, her fair, straight hair falling like a curtain across her cheek. They both looked up and greeted us.

"Bad?" Robbie repeated. "No. Sky didn't strike me as bad. Powerful, yes. Sexy—absolutely." He grinned.

"Who's this?" Jenna asked.

"Sky Eventide," Robbie reported. "She's the blood witch that Bree and Raven have in their new coven. Oh, guess their coven's name." He laughed. "Kithic. It means 'left-handed' in Gaelic. Raven picked out that name from something she read, without knowing what it meant."

The rest of us smiled. After our fight, Bree had split off from Cirrus to start her own coven with Raven. To me it seemed both of them were just playing at being Wiccan, doing it to look cool, to get back at me for winning Cal, or just to do something different. Widow's Vale is a small town, and there aren't that many entertainment opportunities.

Or maybe I was selling them short. Maybe they were really sincere in their commitment. I sighed and rubbed my forehead, feeling like I didn't know anything anymore.

In homeroom people were already planning their Thanksgiving holidays, which would start at noon on Wednesday. It would be a relief not to have to go to school for a few days. I've always been an A student (well, mostly), but it was getting harder and harder to keep my mind on schoolwork when so many more compelling things were taking up my time and energy. Nowadays I just flashed through my physics and trig homework and did the bare minimum in other classes so I would have more time to study spells, plan my future magickal herb garden, and read about Wicca. Not only that, but just reading the Book of Shadows written by my birth mother, which I'd found in Selene's library over a week ago, was like a college course in itself. I was stretched very thin these days.

In homeroom I opened my book *Essential Oils and Their Charms* under my desk and started reading. In the spring I would try to make some of my own, the way Selene did.

When Bree came into class, I couldn't help looking up. Her face was as familiar as my own, but nowadays she had another layer to her, a layer that didn't include me. She wore mostly black, like Raven did, and although she hadn't adopted any of Raven's gothy piercings or tattoos, I wondered if it was just a matter of time.

Bree had always been the beautiful one, the one boys flocked around, the life of the party. I had been the plain friend that people put up with because Bree loved me and was my best friend, but then Cal had come between us. Bree had even lied and told me they'd slept together. We'd quit speaking, and then Cal and I started going out.

After being like conjoined twins for eleven years, I'd found the last few Breeless weeks bizarre and uncomfortable. She still didn't know I was adopted, that I was a blood witch. She didn't know about what had happened with Hunter. At one time she had been the only person in the world I might have told.

I couldn't resist looking at her face, her eyes the color of coffee. For just a second she met my gaze, and I was startled by the mix of emotions there. We both looked away at the same time. Did she miss me? Did she hate me? What was she doing with Sky?

The bell rang, and we all stood. Bree's dark, shiny hair disappeared through the doorway, and I followed her. When she turned the corner to go to her first class, I was seized by a spontaneous desire to talk to her.

"Bree."

She turned, and when she saw it was me, she looked surprised.

"Listen—I know that Sky is leading your coven," I found myself saying.

"So?" No one looked imperious like Bree looked imperious.

"I just—it's just that Sky is dangerous," I said quickly. "She's dangerous, and you shouldn't hang out with her."

Her perfect eyebrows rose. "Do tell," she drawled.

"She has this whole dark agenda; she's caught up in this whole program that I bet she hasn't told you about. She's—she's evil, she's bad, and dangerous." I realized in despair that I sounded melodramatic and muddled.

"Really." Bree shook her head, looking like she was trying not to laugh. "You are too much, Morgan. It's like you get off on lying, raining on people's parades."

"Look, I heard you and Raven last week in the bathroom," I admitted. "You were talking about how Sky was teaching you about the dark side. That's dangerous! And I heard you saying you gave Sky some of my hair! What was that about? Is she putting spells on me?"

Bree's eyes narrowed. "You mean you were spying on me?" she exclaimed. "You're pathetic! And you have no idea what you're talking about. Cal is filling your head with ridiculous crap, and you're just sucking it up! He could be the devil himself, and you wouldn't care because he's the only boy who ever asked you out!"

Before I realized what was happening, my hand had shot out and smacked Bree hard across the face. Her head snapped sideways, and within seconds the pink outline of my palm appeared on her cheek. I gasped and stared at her as her face twisted into anger.

"You bitch!" she snarled.

Out of lifelong habit, I started to feel remorseful, and then I thought, Screw that. I took a deep breath and called on my own anger, narrowing my eyes. "You're the bitch," I snapped. "You can't stand the fact that I'm not your puppet anymore, that I'm not your charity case, your permanent audience. You're jealous of *me* for once, and it's eating you up. I have a fantastic boyfriend, I have more magickal power than you'll ever dream about, and you can't stand it. Finally I'm better than you. I'm amazed your head doesn't explode!"

Bree gaped at me, her eyes wide, her mouth open. "What are you talking about?" she practically shrieked. "You were never my audience! You make it sound like I was using you! This is what I'm talking about! Cal is brainwashing you!"

"Actually, Bree," I said coldly, "you'd be amazed at how little we talk about you. In fact, your name hardly comes up."

With that, I swept off, my teeth clenched so tight, I could feel them grinding together. I didn't think I'd ever had the last word in an argument with Bree before. But the thought didn't make me feel any better. Why had I talked to her? I had just made everything worse.

4.
Haven

May 2000

I remember it rained the day Mum and Dad disappeared. When I woke up that morning they were already gone. I had no idea what was going on. Uncle Beck called late that day, and I told him I couldn't find Dad, or Mum either. Beck called around, to get a neighbor to stay overnight with us until he could get there, and he couldn't find anyone still around. In the end, I was in charge all that long day and night, and the three of us—me, Linden, and Alwyn—stayed in our house alone, not knowing what was happening to us, to our world.

Now I know that twenty-three other people besides my parents either died or disappeared that night. Years later, when I went back, I tried asking around. All I got were cautious mumbles about a dark wave, a cloud of fury and destruction.

I've heard rumors of a dark wave destroying a Wyndenkell

coven in Scotland. I'm on my way there. Goddess, give me strength.

— Giomanach

After my fight with Bree, I was so upset that I couldn't concentrate on anything. My trig teacher had to call my name three times before I responded, and then I answered his question incorrectly—which almost never happened to me under normal circumstances. During lunch period I sneaked off to Cirrus's hangout spot to be by myself. I scarfed down my sandwich and a Diet Coke, then meditated for half an hour. Finally I felt calm enough to deal with the rest of my day.

I slogged through my afternoon classes. When the last bell rang, I went to my locker, then followed the crush of students outside. The snow was turning rapidly to slush, and the sun flowed down with an Indian-summerish warmth. After weeks of freezing weather, it felt wonderful. I raised my face to the sun, hoping it would help heal the pain I carried inside, the guilt over what I'd done to Hunter, the terror of being found out.

"I'm getting a ride home with Bakker, okay?" Mary K. bounced up to me as I took out my car keys, her cheeks flushed pink, her eyes clear and shining.

I looked at her. "Are you going home, or . . ." Don't go anywhere with him alone, I thought. I didn't trust Bakker— not since I'd caught him pinning Mary K. down on her bed and practically forcing himself on her two weeks earlier. I couldn't believe she'd forgiven him.

"We're going to get a latte first, then home," she said, her eyes daring me to say something.

"All right. Well, see you later," I said lamely. I watched her climb into Bakker's car and knew that if he hurt her, I would have no problem doing to him what I had done to Hunter. And in Bakker's case I wouldn't feel guilty.

"Whoa. I'm glad you're not looking at me like that," said Robbie, loping up to me. I shook my head.

"Yeah, just watch your step." I tried to sound light and teasing.

"Is Cal sick? I didn't see him all day," said Robbie. He smiled absentmindedly at a sophomore who was sending flirtatious looks his way.

"Morgan?" he prompted.

"Oh! Um, yes, Cal is sick," I said. I felt a sudden jangle of nerves. Robbie was a close friend, and I had told him about being adopted and a blood witch. He knew more about me than Bree did now. But I could never tell him about all that had happened on Saturday night. It was too horrible to share, even with him. "I'm going to call him right now—maybe go see him."

Robbie nodded. "I'm on my way to Bree's. Who knows, today might be the day I go for it." He wiggled his eyebrows suggestively, and I smiled. Robbie had recently admitted to me that he was totally in love with Bree and had been for years. I hoped she wouldn't break his heart the way she did with most of the guys she got involved with.

"Good luck," I said. He walked off, and I dumped my backpack in Das Boot and headed back to the pay phone in the school lunchroom.

Cal answered after four rings. His voice sounded better than it had the night before.

"Hi," I said, comforted just to talk to him.

"I knew it was you," he said, sounding glad.

"Of course you did," I said. "You're a witch."

"Where are you?"

"School. Can I come see you? I just really need to talk to you."

Groaning, he said, "I would love that. But some people just came in from Europe, and I've got to meet with them."

"Selene's been having people over a lot lately, it seems."

Cal paused, and when he spoke, his voice had a slightly different tone to it. "Yeah, she has. She's kind of been working on a big project, and it's starting to come together. I'll tell you about it later."

"Okay. How are your wrists?"

"They look pretty bad. But they'll be okay. I really wish I could see you," Cal said.

"Me too." I lowered my voice. "I *really* need to talk to you. About what happened."

"I know," he said quietly. "I know, Morgan."

In the background on Cal's end I heard voices, and Cal covered his mouthpiece and responded to them. When he came back on, I said, "I won't keep you. Call me later if you can, okay?"

"I will," he said. Then he hung up. I hung up, too, feeling sad and lonely without him.

I walked through the hall and out the door, got in Das Boot, and drove to Red Kill, to Practical Magick.

*   *   *

The brass bells over the door jingled as I pushed my way in. Practical Magick was a store that sold Wiccan books and supplies. Although I hadn't realized it until now, it was also becoming the place I went to when I didn't want to go anywhere else. I loved being there, and I always felt better when I left. It was like a Wiccan neighborhood bar.

At the end of the room the checkout desk was empty, and I figured Alyce and David must be busy restocking.

I began reading book titles, dreaming of the day I would have enough money to buy whatever books and supplies I wanted. I would buy this whole store out, I decided. That would be so much more fun than being a relatively poor high school junior who was about to wipe out her whole savings to pay for a crumpled headlight.

"Hi, there," came a soft voice, and I looked up to see the round, motherly figure of Alyce, my favorite clerk. As my eyes met hers, she stood still. Her brows drew together in a concerned look. "What's the matter?"

My heart thudded against my ribs. Does she know? I wondered frantically. Can she tell just by looking at me?

"What do you mean?" I asked. "I'm fine. Just a little stressed. You know, school, family stuff." I shut my mouth abruptly, feeling like I was babbling.

Alyce held my gaze for a moment, her eyes probing mine. "All right. If you want to talk about it, I'm here," she said at last.

She bustled over to the checkout counter and began to stack some papers. Her gray hair was piled untidily on top of her head, and she wore her usual loose, flowing clothes. She moved with precision and confidence: a woman at ease with herself, her witchhood, her power. I admired her, and it broke my heart to think how horrified she would be if she knew what I had done. How had this happened? How had this become my life?

I can't lose this, I thought. Practical Magick was my haven. I couldn't let the poison of Hunter's horrible death seep out and taint my relationships with this place, with Alyce. I couldn't bear it.

"I can't wait for spring," I said, trying to get my mind back on track. It wasn't even Thanksgiving yet. "I want to get started on my garden." I walked up the book aisle to the back of the store and leaned against a stool by the counter.

"So do I," Alyce agreed. "I'm already dying to be outside, digging in the dirt again. It's always a struggle for me to remember the positive aspects of winter."

I looked around at the other people in the store. A young man with multiple earrings in his left ear came up and bought incense and white candles. I tentatively sent out my senses to see if I could tell if he was a witch or not, but I couldn't pick up on anything unusual.

"Morgan, good to see you again."

I turned to see David stepping through the faded orange curtain that separated the small back room from the rest of the store. A faint scent of incense wafted in with him. Like Alyce, David was also a blood witch. Recently he'd told me that he was from the Burnhide clan. I felt honored to have gained his confidence—and terrified of losing it again if he ever found out what I'd done, that I'd killed someone.

"Hi," I said. "How are you?"

"I'm all right." He held a sheaf of invoices in his hand and looked distracted. "Alyce, did the latest batch of essential oils come? The bill is here."

She shook her head. "I have a feeling the shipment is lost somewhere," she said as another person checked out. This woman was buying a Wiccan periodical called *Crafting Our Lives*. I picked up on faint magickal vibrations as she passed me and was once again naively amazed that real witches existed.

I wandered around the store, fascinated as always by the candles, incense, small mirrors the shop contained. Slowly the place emptied, then new people came in. It was a busy afternoon.

Gradually the sunlight faded from the high windows, and I began to think about heading home. Alyce came up as I was running my fingers around the rim of a carved marble bowl. The stone was cool and smooth, like river stones. The stones Hunter had probably hit when he fell hadn't been smooth. They had been jagged, deadly.

"Marble is always thirteen degrees cooler than the air around it," Alyce said at my side, making me jump.

"Really? Why?"

"It's the property of the stone," she said, straightening some scarves that customers had rumpled. "Everything has its own properties."

I thought about the chunks of crystal and other stones I had found in the box containing my mother's tools. It seemed like ages ago—but it had actually been less than a week.

"I found Maeve's tools," I said, surprising myself. I hadn't planned to mention it. But I felt the need to confide *something* in Alyce, to make her feel I wasn't shutting her out.

Alyce's blue eyes widened, and she stopped what she was doing to look at me. She knew Maeve's story; it had been she who'd told me of my birth mother's awful death here in America.

"Belwicket's tools?" she asked unbelievingly. Belwicket had been the name of Maeve's coven in Ireland. When it was destroyed by a mysterious, dark force, Maeve and her lover, Angus, had fled to America. Where I'd been born—and they had died.

"I scryed," I told Alyce. "In fire. I had a vision that told me the tools were in Meshomah Falls."

"Where Maeve died," Alyce remembered.

"Yes."

"How wonderful for you," Alyce said. "Everyone thought those tools were lost forever. I'm sure Maeve would have been so happy for her daughter to have them."

I nodded. "I'm really glad about it. They're a link to her, to her clan, her family."

"Have you used them yet?" she asked.

"Um—I tried the athame," I admitted. Technically, since I was uninitiated, I wasn't supposed to do unsupervised magick or use magickal tools or even write in Cirrus's Book of Shadows. I waited for Alyce to chide me.

But she didn't. Instead she said briskly, "I think you should bind the tools to you."

I blinked. "What do you mean?"

"Wait a minute." Alyce hurried off and soon came back with a thick, ancient-looking book. Its cover was dark green and tattered, with stains mottling its fabric. She leaned the book on a shelf and flipped through pages soft and crumbling with age.

"Here we go." She pulled a quaint pair of half-moon glasses from her sweater pocket and perched them on her nose. "Let me copy this down for you." Then, just like the women at my church exchange recipes and knitting patterns, Alyce copied down an age-old Wiccan spell that would bind my mother's tools to me.

"It will be almost as if you're part of them and they are part of you," Alyce explained as I folded the paper and put it in my inside coat pocket. "It will make them more effective for you and also less effective for anyone else who tries to use them. I really think you should do this right away." Her gaze, usually so mild, seemed quite piercing as she examined me over the rims of her glasses.

"Um, okay, I will," I said. "But why?"

Alyce paused for a moment, as if considering what to say. "Intuition," she said finally, shrugging and giving me a smile. "I feel it's important."

"Well, all right," I said. "I'll try to do it tonight."

"The sooner the better," she advised. Then the bells over the door rang as a customer came in. I hastily said good-bye to Alyce and David and went out to Das Boot. I flipped on my one headlight, blasted the heater, and headed for home.

5.
Bound

June 2000

Two covens in Scotland were wiped out: one in 1974 and one in 1985. The first was in the north, the second, toward the southeast. Now the trail is leading into northern England, so I am making plans to go. I have to <u>know</u>. This started out being about my parents. Now it's a much bigger picture.

I've heard that the council is seeking new members. I've put my name in. If I were a council member, I would have access to things that are usually not publicized. It seems the fastest way to have my questions answered. When I come back from the north, I'll learn of their decision.

I applied to become a Seeker. With a name like mine, it seems almost inevitable.

—Giomanach

Mary K. breezed in halfway through dinner. Her cheeks were pink. There was also something wrong with her shirt. I gazed in puzzlement at the two flaps of the hem. They didn't meet—the shirt was incorrectly buttoned. My eyes narrowed as I thought about what that meant.

"Where have you been?" Mom asked. "I was worried."

"I called and let Dad know I'd be late," my sister said, sitting down at the table. Seated, her telltale shirt wasn't so obvious. "What's that?" she asked, sniffing the serving platter.

"Corned beef. I made it in the Crock-Pot," Mom said.

Dad had glanced up at the sound of his name, pulled back to reality for a moment. He's a research-and-development guy for IBM, and sometimes he seems more comfortable in *virtual* reality.

"Hmmm," said Mary K. disapprovingly. She picked out some carrots, cabbage, and onions and conspicuously left the meat. Lately she'd been on a major vegetarian kick.

"It's delicious," I said brightly, just to needle her. Mary K. sent me a look.

"So I think Eileen and Paula have decided on the York Street house, in Jasper," my mom said.

"Cool," I said. "Jasper's only about twenty minutes away, right?" My aunt and her girlfriend had decided to move in together and had been house hunting with my mom, a real estate agent.

"Right," Mom said. "An easy drive from here."

"Good." I stood up and carried my plate to the kitchen, already anxious for my family to be asleep. I had work to do.

The spell for binding tools to oneself was complicated but not difficult, and it didn't involve any tools or ingredients that I didn't have. I knew I would need to work undisturbed, and I didn't want to do it outside. The attic seemed like a good place.

At last I heard my parents turn in and my sister brush her teeth noisily in the bathroom we shared. She poked her head into my room to say good night and found me hunched over a book discussing the differences between practicing Wicca on your own and within a coven. It was really interesting. There were benefits—and drawbacks—to both ways.

"Night," said Mary K., yawning.

I looked at her. "Next time you're late, you might want to make sure your shirt is buttoned right," I said mildly.

She looked down at herself, horrified. "Oh, man," she breathed.

"Just . . . be careful." I wanted to say more but forced myself to stop there.

"Yeah, yeah, I will." She went into her room.

Twenty minutes later, sensing that everyone was asleep, I tiptoed up the attic stairs with Maeve's tools, the spell Alyce had written out for me, and four white candles.

I swept one area clean of dust and set the four candles in a large square. Inside the square I drew a circle with white chalk. Then I entered the circle, closed it, and set Maeve's tools on one of my old sweatshirts. Theoretically, it would be full of my personal vibrations.

I meditated for a while, trying to release my anguish over Hunter, trying to sink into the magick, feeling it unfold before me, gradually revealing its secrets. Then I gathered Maeve's tools: her robe, her wand, her four element cups, her athame, and things I wasn't sure were tools but that I'd found in the same box: a feather, a silver chain with a Claddagh charm on it, several chunks of crystal, and five stones, each one different.

I read the ritual chant.

"Goddess Mother, Protectress of Magick and Life, hear my song. As it was in my clan, so shall it be with me and in my family to come. These tools I offer in service to you and in worship of the glory of nature. With them I shall honor life, do no harm, and bless all that is good and right. Shine your light on these tools that I may use them in pure intent and in sure purpose."

I laid my hands on them, feeling their power and sending mine into them.

The same way it had happened in the past, a song in Gaelic came to my lips. I let it slip quietly into the darkness.

> *"An di allaigh an di aigh*
> *An di allaigh an di ne ullah*
> *An di ullah be nith rah*
> *Cair di na ulla nith rah*
> *Cair feal ti theo nith rah*
> *An di allaigh an di aigh."*

Quietly I sang the ancient words again and again, feeling a warm coil of energy circling me. When I had sung this before, it had drawn down an immense amount of power—I'd felt like a goddess myself. Tonight it was quieter, more focused, and the power flowed around and through me like water, going down my hands into the tools until I couldn't tell where the tools left off and I began. I couldn't feel my knees where I was kneeling, and giddily I wondered if I was levitating.

Suddenly I realized that I was no longer singing and that the warm, rich power had leached away, leaving me breathing hard and flushed, sweat trickling down my back.

I looked down. Were the tools bound to me now? Had I done it correctly? I had followed the instructions. I had felt the power. There was nothing else on the paper Alyce had given me. Blinking, feeling suddenly incredibly tired, I gathered everything up, blew out the candles, and crept downstairs. Moving silently, I unscrewed the cover for the HVAC vent in the hallway outside my room and put my tools, except the athame, back into my never-fail hiding place.

Back in my room, I changed into my pajamas and brushed my teeth. I unbraided my hair and brushed it a few times, too tired to give it any real attention. Finally, with relief, I got into bed with Maeve's Book of Shadows and opened it to my bookmark. Out of habit I held my mother's athame, with its carved initials, in my hand.

I started to read, sometimes pointing the athame to the words on the page, as if it would help me decipher some of the Gaelic terms.

In this entry Maeve was describing a spell to strengthen her scrying. She mentioned that something seemed to be blocking her vision: "It's as if the power lines are clouded and dark. Ma and I have both scryed and scryed, and all we get is the same thing over and over: bad news coming. What that means, I don't know. A delegation is here from Liathach, in northern Scotland. They, like us, are Woodbanes who have renounced evil. Maybe with their help we can figure out what's going on."

I felt a chill. *Bad news coming.* Was it the mysterious dark force that had destroyed Belwicket, Maeve's coven? No, it couldn't be, I realized; that hadn't happened until 1982. This entry had been written in 1981, nearly a year earlier. I tapped the athame against the page and read on.

"I have met a witch."

The words floated across the page, written in light within the regular entry. I blinked and they were gone, and I stared at Maeve's angular handwriting, wondering what I had seen. I focused, staring hard at the page, willing the words, the writing to appear again. Nothing.

I took the athame, passing it slowly over the blue ink. Splashes, pinpricks of light, coalescing into words. "I have met a witch."

I drew in my breath, staring at the page. The words appeared beneath the athame. When I drew it away, they faded. I passed the knife over the book again. "Among the group from Liathach, there is a man. There is something about him. Goddess, he draws me to him."

Oh my God. I looked up, glanced around my room to make sure I was awake and not dreaming. My clock was ticking, Dagda was squirming next to my leg, the wind was blowing against my windows. This was all real. Another layer of my birth mother's history was being revealed: she had written secret entries in her Book of Shadows.

Quickly I flipped to the very beginning of the book, which Maeve had started when she was first initiated at fourteen. Holding the athame close to each page, I scanned the writing, seeing if other hidden messages were revealed. Page after page I ran the knife down each line of writing, each spell, each song or poem. Nothing. Nothing for many, many pages. Then, in 1980, when Maeve was eighteen, hidden words started appearing. I began reading, my earlier fatigue forgotten.

At first the entries were things Maeve had simply wanted to keep hidden from her mother: the fact that she and a girlfriend were smoking cigarettes, about how Angus kept pressuring her to go "all the way" and she was thinking about it, even sarcastic, teasing remarks or observations about people in the village, her relatives, other members of the coven.

But as time went on, Maeve also wrote down spells, spells that were different from the others. A lot of what Maeve and Mackenna and Belwicket had done was practical stuff: healing potions, lucky talismans, spells to make the crops perform. These new spells of Maeve's were things like how to communicate with and call wild birds. How to put your mind into an animal's. How to join your mind to another person's. Not practical, perhaps. But powerful and fascinating.

I went back to the passage I had found a few minutes ago. Slowly, word by word, I read the glowing letters. Each entry was surrounded by runes of concealment and symbols I didn't recognize. I memorized what they looked like so I could research them later.

Painstakingly I picked out the message.

"Ciaran came to tea. He and Angus are circling each other like dogs. Ciaran is a friend, a good friend, and I won't have Angus put him down."

Angus Bramson had been my birth father. Ciaran must be the Scottish witch Maeve had just met. Previous entries had detailed Maeve and Angus's courtship—they'd known each other practically forever. When Belwicket had been destroyed, Maeve and Angus had fled together and settled in America. Two years later I had been born, though I don't think they ever married. Maeve had once written about her sadness that Angus wasn't her *mùirn beatha dàn*—her preordained life partner, her soul mate, the person who was meant for her.

I believed Cal was mine. I'd never felt so close to anyone before—except Bree.

"Today I showed Ciaran the headlands by the Windy Cliffs. It's a beautiful spot, wild and untamed, and he seemed just as wild and untamed as the nature surrounding him. He's so different from the lads around here. He seems older than twenty-two, and he's traveled a bit and seen the world. It makes me ache with envy."

Oh, God, I thought. Maeve, what are you getting into?

I soon found out.

"I cannot help myself. Ciaran is everything a man should be. I love Angus, yes, but he's like a brother to me—I've known him all my life. Ciaran wants the things I want, finds the same things interesting and boring and funny. I could spend days just talking to him, doing nothing else. And then there's his magick—his power. It's breathtaking. He knows so much I don't know, no one around here knows. He's teaching me. And the way he makes me feel . . .

"Goddess! I've never wanted to touch anyone so much."

My throat had tightened and my back muscles had tensed. I rested the book on my knees, trying to analyze why this revelation shook me so much.

Is love ever simple? I wondered. I thought about Mary K.

and Bakker, boy most likely to be a parolee by the time he was twenty; Bree, who went out with one loser after another; Matt, who had cheated on Jenna with Raven. . . . It was completely discouraging. Then I thought about Cal, and my spirits rose again. Whatever troubles we had, at least they were external to our love for each other.

I blinked and realized my eyelids were gritty and heavy. It was very late, and I had to go to school tomorrow. One more quick passage.

"I have kissed Ciaran, and it was like sunlight coming through a window. Goddess, thank you for bringing him to me. I think he is the one."

Wincing, I hid the book and the athame under my mattress. I didn't want to know. Angus was my birth father, the one who had stayed by her, who had died with her. And she had loved someone else! She'd betrayed Angus! How could she be so cruel, my mother?

I felt betrayed, too, somehow, and knowing that I was perhaps being unfair to Maeve didn't help. I turned off my light, plumped my pillow up properly, and went to sleep.

6.
Knowledge

I'm going to have these scars forever. Every time I look at my wrists, I feel rage all over again. Mom has been putting salves on them, but they ache constantly, and the skin will never be the same.

Thank the Goddess Giomanach won't bother us anymore.

—Sgàth

"If you hum that song one more time, I may have to kick you out of the car," I informed my sister the next morning.

Mary K. opened the lid of her mug and took a swig of coffee. "My, we're grumpy today."

"It's natural to be grumpy in the morning." I polished off the last of my Diet Coke and tossed the empty can into a plastic bag I kept for recyclables.

"Tornadoes are natural, but they're not a *good* thing."

I snorted, but secretly I enjoyed the bickering. It felt so . . . normal.

Normal. Nothing would ever be normal again. Not after what Cal and I had done.

There'd been no mention of a body in the river in this morning's paper, either. Maybe he'd sunk to the bottom, I thought. Or snagged on a submerged rock or log. I pictured him in the icy water, his pale hair floating around his face like seaweed, his hands swaying limply in the current. . . . A sudden rush of nausea almost made me retch.

Mary K. didn't notice. She looked through the windshield at the thin layer of clouds blotting out the morning sun. "I'll be glad when vacation starts."

I forced a smile. "You and me both."

I turned onto our school's street and found that all my usual parking spaces were taken. "Why don't you get out here," I suggested, "and I'll go park across the street."

"Okay. Later." Mary K. clambered out of Das Boot and hurried to her group of friends, her breath coming out in wisps. Today it was cold again, with a biting wind.

Across the street was another small parking lot, in back of an abandoned real estate office. Large sycamores surrounded the lot, looking like peeling skeletons, and several shaggy cypresses made it feel sheltered and private—which was why the stoners usually hung out there when the weather was warmer. No one else was around as I maneuvered Das Boot into a space. Wednesday, after school let out at noon, I had an appointment to take it to Unser's Auto Repair to have the headlight repaired.

"Morgan." The melodious voice made me jump. I whirled to see Selene Belltower sitting in her car three spaces away, her window rolled down.

"Selene!" I walked over to her. "What are you doing here? Is Cal okay?"

"He's much better," Selene assured me. "In fact, he's on his way to school right now. But I wanted to talk to you. Can you get in the car for a moment, please?"

I opened the door, flattered by her attention. In so many ways, she was the witch I hoped someday to be: powerful, the leader of a coven, vastly knowledgeable.

I glanced at my watch as I sank into the passenger seat. It was covered with soft brown leather, heated, and amazingly comfortable. Even so, I hoped Selene could sum up what she had to say in four minutes or less since that was when the last bell would ring.

"Cal told me you found Belwicket's tools," she said, looking excited.

"Yes," I said.

She smiled and shook her head. "What an amazing discovery. How did you find them?"

"I saw Maeve in a vision," I said. "She told me where to find them."

Selene's eyebrows rose. "Goodness. You had a vision?"

"Yes. I mean, I was scrying," I admitted, flushing. I didn't know for sure, but I had a feeling scrying was another thing I wasn't supposed to do as an uninitiated witch. "And I saw Maeve and where the tools might be."

"What were you scrying with? Water?"

"Fire."

She sat back, surprised, as if I had just come up with an impossibly high prime number.

"Fire! You were scrying with fire?"

I nodded, self-conscious but pleased at her astonishment. "I like fire," I said. "It . . . speaks to me."

There was a moment of silence, and I started to feel uneasy. I had been bending the rules and following my own path with Wicca practically from the beginning.

"Not many witches scry with fire," Selene told me.

"Why not? It works so well."

"It doesn't for most people," Selene replied. "It's very capricious. It takes a lot of power to scry with fire." I felt her gaze on me and didn't know what to say.

"Where are Maeve's tools now?" Selene asked. I was relieved that she didn't sound angry or disapproving. It felt very intimate in the car, very private, as though what we said here would always be secret.

"They're hidden," I said reassuringly.

"Good," said Selene. "I'm sure you know how very powerful those tools are. I'm glad you're being careful with them. And I just wanted to offer my services, my guidance, and my experience in helping you learn to use them."

I nodded. "Thank you."

"And I would hope, because of our close relationship and your relationship with Cal, that you might want me to see the tools, test them, share my power with them. I'm very strong, and the tools are very strong, and it could be a very exciting thing to put our strengths together."

Just then a familiar gold Explorer rolled into the parking lot. I saw Cal's profile through his smoked window, and my heart leapt. He glanced toward us, pausing for a moment before pulling into a spot and turning off the engine. Eagerly I rolled down my window, and as I did, I heard the morning bell ring.

"Hi!" I said.

He came closer and leaned on the door, looking through the open window. "Hi," he said. His injured wrists were covered by his coat sleeves. "Mom? What are you doing here?"

"I just couldn't wait to talk to Morgan about Belwicket's tools," Selene said with a laugh.

"Oh," said Cal. I was puzzled by the flat tone in his voice. He sounded almost annoyed.

"Um, I feel like I should tell you," I said hesitantly. "I, uh, I bound the tools to me. I don't think they'll work too well for anyone else."

Cal and Selene both stared at me as if I had suddenly announced I was really a man.

"What?" said Selene, her eyes wide.

"I bound the tools to me," I said, wondering if I had acted too hastily. But Alyce had seemed so certain.

"What do you mean, you bound the tools to you?" Cal asked carefully.

I swallowed. I felt suddenly like a kid called in front of the principal. "I did a spell and bound the tools to me, sending my vibrations through them. They're part of me now."

"Whoa. How come?" Cal said.

"Well," I said, "you know, to make it harder for others to use them. And to increase my power when I use them."

"Heavens," said Selene. "Who told you how to do that?"

I opened my mouth to say, "Alyce," but instead, to my surprise, what came out was, "I read about it."

"Hmmm," she said thoughtfully. "Well, there are ways to unbind tools."

"Oh," I said, feeling uncertain. Why would she want me to unbind them?

"I would love to show you some hands-on ways to use them." Selene smiled. "You can't get everything from books."

"No," I agreed. I still felt uncertain and indefinably uneasy. "Well, I'd better get going."

"All right," said Selene. "Congratulations again on finding the tools. I'm so proud of you."

Her words warmed me, and I got out of the car feeling better.

I looked at Cal. "You coming?"

"Yeah," he said. He hesitated as if he were about to say something else, then seemed to change his mind, calling merely, "Talk to you later, Mom."

"Right," she said, and the window rolled up.

Cal set off for school. His strides were so long that I practically had to run to keep up. When I glanced at his profile, I could see that his jaw was set. "What's wrong?" I asked breathlessly. "Are you upset about something?"

He glanced at me. "No," he said. "Just don't want to be late."

But I didn't need my witch senses to see that he was lying. Was he angry at me because I'd bound the tools to me and now no one else could use them?

Or was he angry with Selene? It had almost seemed like he was. But why?

My day went downhill from there. While I was changing classes at fourth period, I accidentally walked in on Matt Adler and Raven Meltzer making out in an empty chem lab. When our eyes met, Matt looked like he wanted to vaporize himself, and Raven looked even more smug than usual. Ugh, I thought. Then it occurred to me that I could never judge anyone again about anything because what I had done was so terrible, so unnatural. And as soon as I thought that, I went into the girls' bathroom and cried.

At lunchtime Cal and I sat with Cirrus at our usual table. The group was quiet today. Robbie was tight faced, and I wondered how it had gone at Bree's house yesterday. Probably not well since Bree was across the lunchroom sitting on Chip Newton's lap and laughing. Great.

Jenna was even paler than usual. When Cal asked her where Matt was, she said, "I wouldn't know. We broke up last night." She shrugged, and that was that. I was surprised and impressed by how calm she seemed. She was stronger than she looked.

Ethan Sharp and Sharon Goodfine were sitting next to each other. After months of flirting, they were looking into each other's eyes as if they'd finally realized the other was a real person and not just a clever simulation. Sharon shared her bagel with him. It was the only cheerful thing that happened.

Somehow I slogged through the afternoon. I kept thinking about Selene teaching me to use Maeve's tools. One minute I would want to do it, and the next minute I would remember Alyce's warning and decide to keep them to myself. I couldn't make up my mind.

When the final bell rang, I gathered up my things with relief. Only half a day tomorrow, thank the Goddess, and then a four-day weekend. I walked outside, looking for Mary K.

"Hey," said my sister, coming up. "Cold enough for

you?" We glanced up at the striated clouds that scudded slowly across the sky.

"Yeah," I said, hitching up my backpack. "Come on. I'm parked over in the side lot."

Just as I turned, Cal came up. "Hey, Mary K.," he said. Then he ducked his head and spoke only to me. "Is it okay if I come over this afternoon?" There was an unspoken message—we had tons to talk about—and I nodded at once.

"I'll meet you there."

He touched my cheek briefly, smiled at Mary K., then walked beside us to his own car. My sister raised an eyebrow at me, and I shot her a glance.

Once we were in Das Boot and I was cranking the engine, Mary K. said, "So, have you done it yet?"

I almost punched the gas, which would have slammed us right into a tree.

"Good God, Mary K.!" I cried, staring at her.

She giggled, then tried to look defiant. "Well? You've been going out a month, and he's gorgeous, and you can tell *he's* not a virgin. You're my sister. If I don't ask you, who can I ask?"

"Ask about what?" I said irritably, backing out.

"About sex," she said.

I rested my head for a second against the steering wheel. "Mary K., this may surprise you, but you're only fourteen years old. You're a high school freshman. Don't you think you're too young to worry about this?"

As soon as the words were out of my mouth, I wished I could take them back. I sounded just like my mom. I wasn't surprised when my sister's face closed.

"I'm sorry," I said. "You just . . . took me by surprise. Give me a second." I tried to think quickly and drive at the same time. "Sex." I blew out my breath. "No, I haven't done it yet."

Mary K. looked surprised.

I sighed. "Yes, Cal wants to. And I want to. But it hasn't seemed exactly right yet. I mean, I love Cal. He makes me feel unbelievable. And he's totally sexy and all that." My cheeks heated. "But still, it's only been a month, and there's a lot of other stuff going on, and it just . . . hasn't seemed right." I frowned at her pointedly. "And I think it's really important to wait until it *is* exactly right, and you're totally comfortable and sure and crazy in love. Otherwise it's no good." Said the incredibly experienced Morgan Rowlands.

Mary K. looked at me. "What if the other person *is* sure and you just want to trust them?"

Note to self: Do a castration spell on Bakker Blackburn. I breathed in, turned onto our street, and saw Cal in back of us. I pulled into our driveway and turned off the engine but stayed in the car. Cal parked and walked up to the house, waiting for us on the porch.

"I think you know enough to be sure for yourself," I said quietly. "You're not an idiot. You know how you feel. Some people date for years before they're both ready to have sex." Where was I getting this stuff? Years of reading teen magazines?

"The important thing," I went on, "is that you make your own decisions and don't give in to pressure. I told Cal I wasn't ready, and he was majorly disappointed." I lowered my voice as if he could hear us from twenty feet away, outside the car. "I mean, *majorly*. But he accepted my decision and is waiting until I'm ready."

Mary K. looked at her lap.

"However, if for some reason you think it might happen, for God's sake use nine kinds of birth control and check out his health and be careful and don't get hurt. Okay?"

My sister blushed and nodded. On the porch I saw Cal shifting his feet in the cold.

"Do you want me to send Cal home so we can talk some more?" Please say no.

"No, that's okay," said Mary K. "I think I get it."

"Okay. I'm always here. I mean, if you can't ask your sister, who can you ask?"

She grinned, and we hugged each other. Then we hurried inside. Twenty minutes later Mary K. was doing her homework upstairs and Cal and I were drinking hot tea in the kitchen. And I hoped my sister had taken my words to heart.

7.
Self

July 2000

The council called me to London upon my return from the North. I spent three days answering questions about everything from the causes of the Clan wars to the medic- inal properties of mugwort. I wrote essays analyzing past decisions of the elders. I performed spells and rituals.

And then they turned me down. Not because my power is weak or my knowledge scanty, nor yet because I am too young, but because they distrust my motives. They think I am after vengeance for Linden, for my parents.

But that's not it, not anymore. I spoke to Athar about it last night. She's the only one who truly understands, I think.

"You aren't after vengeance. You're after redemption," she told me, and her black eyes measured me. "But, Giomanach, I'm not sure which is the more dangerous quest."

She's a deep one, my cousin Athar. I don't know when she grew to be so wise.

I won't give up. I will write to the council again today. I'll make them understand.

—Giomanach

Our kitchen was about one-sixth the size of Cal's kitchen, and instead of granite counters and custom country French cabinets, we had worn Formica and cabinets from about 1983. But our kitchen felt homier.

I rested my legs over Cal's knees under the table and we leaned toward each other, talking. The idea that maybe someday we would have our very own house, just us two, made me shiver. I looked up at Cal's smooth tan skin, his perfect nose, his strong eyebrows, and sighed. We needed to talk about Hunter.

"I'm really shaken up," I said quietly.

"I know. I am, too. I never thought it would come to that." He gave a dry laugh. "Actually, I thought we would just beat each other up a bit, and the whole thing would blow over. But when Hunter pulled out the braigh—"

"The silver chain he was using?"

Cal shuddered. "Yes," he said, his voice rough. "It was spelled. Once it was on me, I was powerless."

"Cal, I just can't believe what happened," I said, my eyes filling with tears. I brushed them away with one hand. "I can't think about anything else. And why hasn't anyone found the body yet? What are we going to do when they do find it? I swear, every time the phone rings, I think it's going to be the police, asking me to come down to the station and answer some questions." A tear overflowed and ran down my cheek. "I just can't get over this."

"I'm so sorry." Cal pushed his chair closer to mine and put his arms around me. "I wish we were at my house," he said quietly. "I just want to hold you without worrying about your folks coming in."

I nodded, sniffling. "What are we going to do?"

"There's nothing we can do, Morgan," Cal said, kissing my temple. "It was horrible, and I've cursed myself a thousand times for involving you in it. But it happened, and we can't take it back. And never forget that we acted in self-defense. Hunter was trying to kill me. You were trying to protect me. What else could we have done?"

I shook my head.

"I've never been through anything like this before," Cal said softly against my hair. "It's the worst thing in my life. But you know what? I'm glad I'm going through it with you. I mean, I'm sorry you were involved. I wish to the Goddess that you weren't. But since we were in it together, I'm so glad I have you." He shook his head. "This isn't making sense. I'm just trying to say that in an awful way, this has made me feel closer to you."

I looked up into his eyes. "Yeah, I know what you mean."

We stayed like that, sitting at the table, our arms around each other, until my shoulder blades began to ache from the angle and I reluctantly pulled away. I had to change the subject.

"Your mom seemed really excited about my tools," I said, taking a sip of my tea.

Cal pushed his hands through his raggedy dark hair. "Yeah. She's like a little kid—she wants to get her hands on every new thing. Especially something like Belwicket's tools."

"Is there something special about Belwicket in particular?"

Cal shrugged, looking thoughtful. He sipped his tea and said, "I guess just the mystery of it—how it was destroyed, and how old the coven was and how powerful. It's a blessing the tools weren't lost. Oh, and they were Woodbane," he added as an afterthought.

"Does it matter that they were Woodbane since Belwicket had renounced evil?"

"I don't know," said Cal. "Probably not. I think it probably matters more what you *do* with your magick."

I breathed in the steam from my tea. "Maybe I bound the tools to me without thinking it through too well," I said. "What would happen if another witch tried to use them now?"

Cal shrugged. "It's not predictable. Another witch might subvert the tools' power in an unexpected way. Actually, it's pretty unusual for someone to bind a coven's tools only to themselves." He looked up and met my glance.

"I just felt they were mine," I said lamely. "Mine, my birth mother's, her mother's. I wanted them to be all mine."

Nodding, Cal patted my leg, across his knee. "I'd probably do the same thing if they were mine," he said, and I adored him for his support.

"And then Mom would kill me," he added, laughing. I laughed, too.

"Your mom said I was an unusually powerful witch, this morning in the car," I said. "So witches have different strengths of power? In one of my Wiccan history books it talks about some witches being more powerful than others. Does that mean that they just know more, or does it mean something about their innate power?"

"Both," Cal said. He put his feet on either side of mine under the table. "It's like regular education. How accomplished you are depends on how intelligent you are as well as how much education you have. Of course, blood witches are always going to be more powerful than humans. But even among blood witches there's definitely a range. If you're naturally a weak witch, then you can study and practice all you want and your powers will be only so-so. If you're a naturally powerful witch, yet don't know anything about Wicca, you can't do much, either. It's the combination that matters."

"Well, how strong is your mother, for example?" I asked. "On a scale of one to ten?"

Laughing, Cal leaned across and kissed my cheek. "Careful. Your math genes are showing."

I grinned.

"Let's see," he mused. He rubbed his chin, and I saw a flash of bandage on his wrist. My heart ached for the pain he had gone through. "My mother, on a scale of one to ten. Let's make it a scale of one to a hundred. And a weak witch without much training would be about a twelve."

I nodded, putting this mythical person on the scale.

"And then someone like, oh, Mereden the Wise or Denys Haraldson would be up in the nineties."

I nodded, recognizing the names Mereden and Denys from my Wiccan history books. They had been powerful witches, role models, educators, enlighteners. Mereden had been burned at the stake back in 1517. Denys had died in 1942 in a London bomb blitz.

"My mom is about an eighty or an eighty-five on that scale," Cal said.

My eyes widened. "Wow. That's way up there."

"Yep. She's no one to mess with," Cal said wryly.

"Where are you? Where am I?"

"It's harder to tell," Cal said. He glanced at his watch. "You know, it'll be dark soon, and I'd really like to put some spells on your house and car while Sky's still in town."

"Okay," I agreed, standing up. "But you really can't say where we are on the Cal scale of witch power? Which reminds me: is it Calvin or just Cal?"

He laughed and brought his mug over to the sink. From upstairs we heard Mary K. blasting her latest favorite CD. "It's Calhoun," he said as we walked into the living room.

"Calhoun," I said, trying it out. I liked it. "Answer my question, Calhoun."

"Let me think," said Cal, putting on his coat. "It's hard to be objective about myself—but I think I'm about a sixty-two. I mean, I'm young; my powers will likely increase as I get older. I'm from good lines, I'm a good student, but I'm not a shooting star. I'm not going to take the Wiccan world by storm. So I'd give myself about a sixty-two."

I laughed and hugged him through his coat. He put his arms around me and stroked my hair down my back. "But you," he said quietly, "you are something different."

"What, like a twenty?" I said.

"Goddess, no," he said.

"Thirty-five? Forty?" I made my eyes look big and hopeful. It made me happy to tease and joke with Cal. It was so easy to love him, to be myself, and to like who I was with him.

He smiled slowly, making me catch my breath at his beauty. "No, sweetie," he said gently. "I think you're more like a ninety. Ninety-five."

Startled, I stared at him, then realized he was joking. "Oh, very funny," I said, laughing. I pulled away and put on my own coat. "We can't *all* be magickal wonders. We can't *all* be—"

"You're a shooting star," he said. His face was serious, even grave. "You *are* a magickal wonder. A prodigy. You could take the Wiccan world by storm."

I gaped, trying to make sense of his words. "What are you talking about?"

"It's why I've been trying to get you to go slowly, not rush things," he said. "You have a tornado inside you, but you have to learn to control it. Like with Maeve's tools. I wish you'd let my mother guide you. I'm worried that you might be getting into something over your head because you're not seeing the big picture."

"I don't know what you mean," I said uncertainly.

He smiled again, his mood lightening, and dropped a kiss on my lips. "Oh, it's no big deal," he said with teasing sarcasm. "It's just, you know, you have a power that comes along every couple of generations. Don't worry about it."

Despite my confusion, Cal really wouldn't talk about it anymore. Outside, he concentrated on spelling Das Boot and my house with runes and spells of protection, and once that was done, he went home. And I was left with too many questions.

That night after dinner my parents took Mary K. to her friend Jaycee's violin recital. Once they were gone, I locked all the doors, feeling melodramatic. Then I went upstairs, took out Maeve's tools, and went into my room.

Sitting on my floor, I examined the tools again. They felt natural in my hands, comfortable, an extension of myself. I wondered what Cal had meant about not seeing the big picture. To me, the big picture was: these had been my grandmother's tools, then my mother's; now they were mine. Any other big picture was secondary to that.

Still, I was sure Selene could teach me a lot about them. It was a compelling idea. I wondered again why Alyce had urged me to bind them to myself so quickly.

I was halfway through making a circle before I realized what I was doing. With surprise, I looked up to find a piece of chalk in my hand and my circle half drawn. My mother's green silk robe, embroidered with magickal symbols, stars, and runes, was draped over my clothes. A candle burned in the fire cup, incense was in the air cup, and the other two cups held earth and water. Cal's silver pentacle was warm at my throat. I hadn't taken it off since he'd given it to me.

The tools wanted me to use them. They wanted to come alive again after languishing, unused and hidden, for so long. I felt their promise of power. Working quickly, I finished casting my circle. Then, holding the athame, I blessed the Goddess and the God and invoked them.

Now what?

Scrying.

I looked into the candle flame, concentrating and relaxing at the same time. I felt my muscles ease, my breathing slow, my thoughts drift free. Words came to my mind, and I spoke them aloud.

> *"I sense magick growing and swelling.*
> *I visit knowledge in its dwelling.*
> *For me alone these tools endure,*
> *To make my magick strong and sure."*

Then I thought, I am ready to see, and then . . . things started happening.

I saw rows of ancient books and knew these were texts I needed to study. I knew I had years of circles ahead of me, years of observing and celebrating the cycles. I saw myself, bent and sobbing, and understood that the road would not be easy. Exhilarated, I said, "I'm ready to see more."

Abruptly my vision changed. I saw an older me leaning over a cauldron, and I looked like a children's cartoon of a witch, with long, stringy hair, bad skin, sunken cheeks, hands like claws. It was so horrible, I almost giggled nervously. That other me was conjuring, surrounded by sharp-edged, dripping wet stone, as if I stood in a cave by a sea. Outside, lightning flashed and cracked into the cave, shining on the walls, and my face was contorted with the effort of working magick. The cave was glowing with power, that other Morgan was giddy with power, and the whole scene felt awful, bizarre, frightening, yet somehow seductive.

I swallowed hard and blinked several times, trying to

bring myself out of it. I couldn't get enough air and was dimly aware that I was gaping like a fish, trying to get more oxygen to my brain. When I blinked again, I saw sunlight and another, older Morgan walking through a field of wheat, like one of those corny shampoo commercials. I was pregnant. There was no dramatic power around me, no ecstatic conjuring, just peace and quiet and calm.

Now I was breathing quickly, and every time my eyes closed, I alternated between the two images, the two Morgans. I became aware of a deep-seated pain in my chest and throat, and I started to feel panicky and out of control.

I want to get out of this, I thought. I want to get out. Let me *out!*

Somehow I managed to wrench my gaze away from the candle flame, and then I was leaning over, gasping on my carpet, feeling dizzy and sick. I was flooded with sensation, with memories and visions I couldn't interpret or even see clearly, and suddenly I knew that I was about to vomit. I staggered to my feet, breaking my circle, and lurched drunkenly to the bathroom. I yanked off my robe, slid across the tiled wall until I hovered over the toilet, and then I threw up, almost crying with misery.

I don't know how long I was in there, but it was a long while, and finally I started to cry, aching, deep sobs. I sat there till the sobs subsided, then shakily got to my feet, flushed the toilet, and crept to the sink. Splashing my face with cold water helped, and I brushed my teeth and washed my face again and changed into my pajamas. I felt weak and hollow, as if I had the flu.

Back in my room, Dagda sat in the middle of the broken circle, gazing meditatively at the candle. "Hi, boy," I whispered, then cupped my hand and blew out the candle. My hands trembling, I dismantled everything, storing the tools in their metal box, folding my mother's robe, which seemed alive, crackling with energy. The very air in my room felt charged and unhealthy. I flung open a window, welcoming the twenty-five-degree chill.

I vacuumed up my circle and hid the toolbox again, spelling the HVAC vent with runes of secrecy. Soon after that, the front door opened and I heard my parents' voices. The phone rang at the same moment. I sprang over to the hall extension and said breathlessly, "Hi. I'm glad you called."

"Are you okay?" Cal said. "I suddenly got a weird feeling about you."

He would not be thrilled to hear about my using my mother's tools in a circle. Lack of experience, lack of knowledge, lack of supervision. And so on.

"I'm okay," I said, trying to slow my breathing. I did feel much better, though still a bit shaky. "I just—missed you."

"I miss you, too," he said quietly. "I wish I could be there with you at night."

A cool breeze from my room gave me a quick shiver. "That would be wonderful," I said.

"Well, it's late," he said. "Sleep tight. Think of me when you're lying there."

I felt his voice in the pit of my stomach, and my hand tightened on the phone.

"I will," I whispered as Mary K. started coming upstairs loudly.

"Good night, my love."

"Good night."

8.
Symbols

September 2000

I'm in Ireland. I went to the town of Ballynigel, where the Belwicket coven once was. It was wiped out around Imbolc in 1982, along with most of the town. So far it's the only Woodbane coven I've found that the dark wave has destroyed. But everyone knows Belwicket renounced evil back in the 1800s and had kept to the council's laws since the laws were first written. Did that have something to do with it? When I stood there and saw the bits of riven earth and charred stones that are all that's left, it made my heart ache.

Tonight I am meeting with Jeremy Mertwick, from the second ring of the council. I have written them a letter every week, appealing their decision. I still hope to make them see reason. I am strong and sure, and my pain has made me older than they know.

—Giomanach

"C'mon, last day before break," Mary K. coaxed, standing over my bed. She waved a warm Toaster Strudel under my nose. I sat up, patted Dagda, and then staggered unhappily to the shower.

"Five minutes," Mary K. called in warning. Then I heard her say, "Come on, little guy. Auntie Mary K. will feed you."

Her voice faded as the hot spray needled down my skin, making me feel semihuman.

Downstairs, my sister handed me a Diet Coke. "Robbie called. His car won't start. We need to pick him up on the way."

We headed out and detoured over to Robbie's house. He was waiting out front, leaning against his red Volkswagen.

"Battery dead again?" I greeted him as he climbed into Das Boot's backseat.

He nodded glumly. "Again." We drove on in companionable morning silence.

At school Mary K. was met as usual by Bakker.

"Young love," Robbie said dryly, watching them nuzzle.

"Ugh," I said, turning off the engine.

"Thanks for the ride," Robbie said. Something in his voice made me turn and look at him.

"So I kissed Bree on Monday," he said.

I sat back, taking my hand off the door handle. I had been so wrapped up in my own misery that I had forgotten to check in with Robbie about Bree. "Wow," I said, examining his face. "I wondered what had happened. I, um, I saw her yesterday with Chip."

Robbie nodded, scanning the school grounds through the car window. He said nothing, and I prompted him: "So?"

He shrugged, his broad shoulders moving inside his army surplus parka. He gave a short laugh. "She let me kiss her. It blew my mind. She just laughed and seemed into it, and I thought, All *right*. And then I came up for air and said that I loved her." He stopped.

"And?" I practically screeched.

"She wasn't into *that*. Dropped me like a stone. Practically pushed me out the door." He rubbed his forehead, as if he had a headache. Silently I offered him my soda, and he finished it off and wiped his mouth with the back of his hand.

"Hmmm," I said. I didn't trust Bree anymore. Before, she might have done the same thing to Robbie, but now I couldn't help wondering how her involvement in Kithic had affected her actions.

"Yeah. Hmmm."

"But the making out worked?" I asked.

"Worked fabulously. Hot, hot, hot." He couldn't help grinning at the memory.

"Okay, I don't need to know," I said quickly.

I took a minute to think. Was Bree capable of using Robbie for some dark purpose, or was she just toying with him in her usual way? I didn't know. I decided to take a chance.

"Well, my advice to you is," I said, "just make out with her. Don't talk to her about your feelings. Not yet, anyway."

He frowned. Outside the car, we saw Cal crunching toward us through the leftover snow, his breath puffing like a dragon's. As usual, my heart lurched when I saw him.

"Hey, I *love* her. I don't want to use her like that."

"No. My point is, let *her* use *you* like that."

"Like a boy toy?" He sounded outraged, but I saw a fleeting interest cross his face.

"Like someone who knocks her off her feet," I pointed out. "Someone who gives her something she can't get from Chip Newton or anyone else."

Robbie stared at me. "You are *ruthless*." I heard admiration in his voice.

"I want you to be happy," I said firmly.

"I think, deep down, you want *her* to be happy, too," Robbie said, unfolding his long frame from the backseat. "Hey, Cal," he said, before I could respond to his remark.

Cal leaned into the open door. "Getting out anytime soon?"

I looked at him. "How about you get in, we take off, and just keep driving until we run out of gas?" I checked my gauge. "Got a full tank." I was only half joking.

When I glanced up, I was startled by the look in his eyes. "Don't tempt me," he said, his voice rough. For a long moment I hung there, suspended in time, pinned by the fierce look of desire and longing. I remembered how it had felt, making out on his bed, touching each other, and I shuddered.

"Hey, Cal," said Ethan from the sidewalk, waving at us as he went into the building.

Cal sighed. "Guess we better go in."

I nodded, not trusting myself to speak.

Cal and I joined the other Cirrus members at the top of the basement stairs.

"Talk about brutal weather," said Jenna as we walked up. She hugged her Nordic sweater closely around her, looking ethereal. I wondered how her asthma was lately and if I could use my tools to help her breathing.

"It's not even officially winter yet. This is the third-coldest autumn on record," Sharon complained, and snuggled closer to Ethan, who looked pleased. Hiding a smile, I sank down on a step, and Cal sat next to me and twined his hand through mine.

"Oh, this is cozy," said Raven's voice. Her dark head appeared over the staircase, followed by another dark head: Matt's. He sat down on a step, the picture of guilt, and she stood there smiling down at us, the Wicked Witch of the Northeast.

"Hi, Raven," said Cal, and she looked him up and down with her shining black eyes.

"Hello, Cal," she drawled. "Having a coven meeting?" She didn't bother lowering her voice, and some students walking past glanced up, startled. And this was Bree's new best friend.

"How's *your* coven going?" I heard myself ask. "Everything okay with Sky?"

Raven's eyes focused on me. Her silver nose ring glinted, her full lips were painted a rich purple, and I was struck by her presence: she was bizarre and luxurious, silly and compelling at the same time.

"Don't talk about Sky," Raven said. "She's a better witch than you'll ever be. You have no idea what you're up against." She stroked two fingers along Matt's smooth cheek, making him flinch, and walked off.

"Well, that was fun," said Robbie when she was gone.

"Matt, why don't you just join Kithic?" Jenna said abruptly, her jaw tight.

Matt frowned, not raising his eyes. "I don't want to," he mumbled.

"Okay, we only have a minute," said Cal, getting down to business. "We have a circle coming up this Saturday, our first in two weeks, and I have an assignment for you."

"I'm sorry, Cal, I won't be here," said Sharon.

"That's okay," he said. "I know you have plans with your family. Do these exercises on your own, and tell us about it the next time we see you. Now, one of the basic platforms of Wicca is self-knowledge. One of my teachers once said, 'Know yourself, and you know the universe,' and that may have been overstating it a bit, but not entirely."

Jenna and Sharon nodded, and I saw Ethan gently massaging Sharon's shoulder.

"I want you to work on self-imaging," Cal went on. "You're going to find your personal correspondences, your own . . . what's the word? I guess *helpers* or *connectors* sort of comes close. They're the things that speak to you, that feel like you, that awaken something in you. Objects or symbols that strengthen your connection to your own magick."

"Not following you here," said Robbie.

"Sorry—let me give you some examples. Things like stones, the four elements, flowers, animals, herbs, seasons, foods," said Cal, ticking them off on his fingers. "My stone is a tigereye. I often use it in my rituals. My element is fire. My metal is gold. My personal rune is—a secret. My season is autumn. My sign is Gemini. My cloth is linen."

"And your car of choice is Ford," Robbie said, and Cal laughed.

"Right. No, seriously. Think especially about elements, stars, stones, seasons, and plants. Define yourselves, but don't limit yourselves. Don't force anything. If nothing speaks to you, don't worry about it. Just move on to something else. But explore your connection to earthly things and to unearthly things." Cal looked around at us. "Any questions?"

"This is so cool," said Sharon.

"I already know your correspondences," Ethan told her. "Your metal is gold, your stone is a diamond, your season is the post-Christmas sale season . . . ouch!" he said as Sharon clipped him smartly on the head. He laughed and raised his hands to defend himself.

"Very funny!" said Sharon, trying not to smile. "And your element is *dirt,* and your metal is *lead,* and your plant is *marijuana!*"

"I don't smoke anymore!" Ethan protested.

We were all laughing, and I felt almost lighthearted in a way that I hadn't since Hunter—

The first bell rang, and suddenly the halls were filled with students swarming to their homerooms. We gathered our various belongings and went our separate ways. And I wondered how much longer I could take this inner darkness.

After the school bell rang at noon, I waited for Cal and Mary K. by the east entrance. It was snowing again. Footsteps sounded behind me, and I turned to see Raven and Bree heading toward the double doors. Bree's face hardened when she saw me.

"So, what are you guys doing for Thanksgiving?" I blinked in surprise as the words left my mouth. Two pairs of dark eyes locked in on me as if I were glowing like a neon light.

"Um, well, gee," Raven said. "I guess I'm celebrating a day of wonder and thankfulness in the arms of my loving family. How about you?"

Since I knew her loving family consisted of a mother who had too many boyfriends and an older brother who was away in the army, I guessed she didn't have plans.

I shrugged. "Family. Turkey. A pumpkin pie gone wrong. Keeping my cat off the dining-room table."

"You have a cat?" Bree asked, unable to help herself. She had a major weakness for cats.

I nodded. "A gray kitten. He's incredibly adorable. Totally bad. Bad and adorable."

"This is delightful"—Raven sighed as Bree opened her mouth to speak—"but we really must be going. We have things to do, people to see."

"Sky?" I asked.

"None of your business," Raven said with a smirk.

Bree was silent as they thumped down the stairs in their matching heavy boots.

A second later Mary K. ran up to say she was going to Jaycee's and Mom had said it was okay, and then Cal came up and asked if I could come over and of course I wanted to. I called Unser's Auto Shop and canceled Das Boot's repair appointment. Then I followed Cal to his house, where we could be alone.

Cal's room was wonderful. It ran the whole length and breadth of the big house since it was the attic. Six dormer windows made cozy nooks, bookcases lined the walls, and he had his own fireplace and an outside staircase leading down to the back patio. His bed was wide and romantic looking, with white bed linens and a gauzy mosquito net looped out of the way. The dark wooden desk where he did his homework had rows of cream-colored candles lining its edge. I had never been in here without envying him this magickal space.

"Want some tea?" he asked, gesturing to the electric kettle. I nodded, and we didn't speak, enjoying the silence and safety of his room.

Two minutes later Cal put a cup of tea into my hand, and I adjusted its temperature and took a sip. "Mmm."

Cal turned away and stood looking out the window. "Morgan," he said. "Forgive me."

"For what?" I asked, raising my eyebrows.

"I lied to you," he said quietly, and my heart clutched in panic.

"Oh?" I marveled at how calm my voice sounded.

"About my clan." The words had almost no sound.

My heart skipped a beat, and I stared at him. He turned to me, his beautiful golden eyes holding promises of love, of passion, of a shared future. And yet his words . . .

He took a sip of tea. The pale light from the window outlined the planes of his cheekbones, the line of his jaw. I waited, and he came close to me, so that his shirt was almost brushing mine and I could see the fine texture of his skin.

Cal turned toward the window again and pushed his fingers through his hair, holding it back from his left temple. I caught a glimpse of a birthmark there, beneath the hair. I reached up and traced its outline with my fingers. It was a dark red athame, just like the one I had under my arm. The mark of the Woodbane clan.

"Hunter was right," Cal went on, his voice low. "I am Woodbane. And I've always known it."

I needed to sit down. I had been so upset when I first found out about my heritage, and Cal had said it wasn't so terrible. Now I saw why. I put down my tea and walked across the room to the futon couch. I sank onto it, and he came to kneel at my side.

"My father was Woodbane, and so is my mother," he said, looking more uncomfortable than I'd ever seen him. "They're not the Belwicket kind of Woodbanes, where everyone renounces evil and swears to do good." He shrugged, not looking at me. "There's another kind of Woodbane, who practices magick traditionally, I mean traditionally for their clan. For Woodbanes that means not being so picky about how you get your knowledge and why you use your power. Traditional Woodbanes don't subscribe to the council's edict that witches never interfere with humans. They figure, humans interfere with us, we all live in the same world, not two separate universes, so they're going to use their powers to take care of problems they might have with humans, or to protect themselves, or to get what they need. . . ."

I was unable to take my eyes off his face.

"After my dad married my mother, I think they started to go different ways, magickally," Cal continued. "Mom has always been very powerful and ambitious, and I think my father disagreed with some of the things she was doing."

"Like what?" I asked, a little shocked.

He waved an impatient hand. "You know, taking too many risks. Anyway, then my dad met Fiona, his second wife. Fiona was a Wyndenkell. I don't know if he wanted a Wyndenkell alliance or he just loved her more. But either way, he left my mother."

I was finally getting some answers. "But if Hunter was right and your father was also *his* father, then wasn't he half Woodbane himself?" This sounded like some awful soap opera. *The Young and the Wiccan.*

"That's the thing," said Cal. "Of course he was. So it made no sense for him to persecute Woodbanes. But he seemed to have a thing about them, like Mom said. An obsession. I wondered if he blamed my father—our father—for what happened to his parents and their coven, for some reason, and so decided to get all Woodbanes. Who knows? He was unhinged."

"So you're Woodbane," I said, still trying to take it all in.

"Yes," he admitted.

"Why didn't you tell me before? I was *hysterical* about being Woodbane."

"I know," he said, sighing. "I should have. But Belwicket was a different kind of Woodbane, a completely good Woodbane, above reproach. I wasn't sure you would understand my family's heritage. I mean, it isn't like they're all evil. They don't worship demons or anything like that. It's just—they do what they want to do. They don't always follow rules."

"Why are you telling me now?"

At last he looked at me, and I felt the pull of his gaze. "Because I love you. I trust you. I don't want any secrets to come between us. And—"

The door to his room suddenly flew open. I jumped about a foot in the air. Selene stood there, dressed beautifully in a dark gold sweater and tweed pants.

Cal stood with swift grace. "What the hell are you doing?"

I had never heard anyone speak to their mother this way, and I flinched.

"What are *you* doing?" she countered. "I felt—what are you talking about?"

"None of your business," he said, and Selene's eyes flashed with surprise.

"We discussed this," she said in a low voice.

"Mom, you need to leave," Cal said flatly. I was embarrassed and confused and also worried: no way did I want to get in between these two if they were fighting.

"How—how did you know he was telling me anything?" I ventured.

"I felt it," Selene said. "I felt him say Woodbane."

This was really interesting. Creepy, but interesting.

"Yes, you're Woodbane," I said, standing up. "I'm Woodbane, too. Is there a reason I shouldn't know your clan?"

"Mom, I trust Morgan, and you need to trust me," Cal said thinly. "Now, will you get back to your work and leave us alone, or do I have to spell the door?"

My lips curved into an involuntary smile, and a second later the tension on Selene's face broke. She breathed out. "Very nice. Threaten your mother," she said tartly.

"Hey, I'll make it so you'll *never* find your way up here again," Cal said, his hands on his hips. He was smiling now, but I felt he wasn't entirely joking. I thought of Selene walking in on us when we were rolling around on Cal's bed and secretly decided maybe spelling the door wouldn't be such a bad idea.

"Forgive me," Selene said at last. "I'm sorry. It's just—Woodbanes have a terrible reputation. We're used to guarding our privacy fiercely. For a moment I forgot who Cal was talking to—and how extraordinary and trustworthy you are. I'm sorry."

"It's okay," I said, and Selene turned around and left. Quickly Cal stepped to the door and snapped the lock behind her, then traced several sigils and runes around the frame of the door with his fingers, muttering something.

"Okay," he said. "That will keep her out." He sounded smug, and I smiled.

"Are you sure?"

The answering look he gave me took my breath away. When he held out his hand, I went to him immediately, and next we tumbled onto his wide bed, the white comforter billowing cozily beneath us. For a long time we kissed and held each other, and I knew that I felt even closer to him than before. Each time we were alone together, we went a little further, and today I needed to feel close to him, needed to be comforted by his touch. Restlessly I pushed my hands under his shirt, against his smooth skin.

I never wore a bra, having a distinct lack of need, and when his hands slipped under my shirt and unerringly found their way to my breasts, I almost cried out. One part of my mind hoped the spell on his door was really foolproof; the other part of my mind turned to tapioca.

I pulled him tightly to me, feeling his desire, hearing his breathing quicken in my ear, amazed at how much I loved him.

This time it was Cal who gradually slowed, who eased the fierceness of his kisses, who calmed his breathing and so made me calm mine. Apparently today would not be the day, either. I was both relieved and disappointed.

After our breathing had more or less returned to normal, he stroked my hair away from my face and said, "I have something to show you."

"Huh?" I said. But he was rolling off the bed, straightening his clothing.

Then he held out his hand to me. "Come," he said, and I followed him without question.

9.
Secrets

It's odd to be the son of a famous witch. Everyone watches you, from the time you can walk and talk—watches you for signs of genius or of mediocrity. You're never offstage.

Mom raised me as she saw fit. She has plans for me, my future. I've never really discussed them with her, only listened to her tell me about them. Until recently, it never crossed my mind to disagree. It's flattering to have someone prepare you for greatness, sure of your ability to pull it off.

Yet since my love came into my life, I feel differently. She questions things, she stands up for herself. She's so naive but so strong, too. She makes me want things I've never wanted before.

I remember back in California—I was sixteen. Mom had started a coven. It was the usual smoke and mirrors—Mom using her circle's powers as sort of an energy boost so she wouldn't have to deplete her own—but then to our surprise she unearthed a very strong witch, a woman about twenty-five or so, who had no idea of her bloodlines. During circles she blew us away. So Mom asked me to get close to her. I did—it was surprisingly easy. Then Mom extinguished her during the Rite of Dubh Siol. It upset me, even though I'd known that it might happen.

It won't come to that this time. I'll make sure.

—Sgàth

As Cal led me down his outside steps to the back patio, the last flakes of falling snow brushed my face and landed on my hair. I held tightly to the iron rail; the metal stairs were slick with snow and ice.

Cal offered me his hand at the bottom of the stair. I crunched onto the snow, and he began to lead me across the stone patio. We were both cold; our coats had been in the downstairs foyer, and we hadn't gotten them.

I realized we were heading toward the pool. "Oh, God, you can't be thinking about going skinny dipping!" I said, only half joking.

Cal laughed, throwing back his head as he led me past the big pool. "No. It's covered for the winter, underneath that snow. Of course, if you're willing . . ."

"I'm not," I said quickly. I had been the lone holdout from a group swim at our coven's second meeting.

He laughed again, and then we were at the little building that served as the pool house. Built to look like a miniature version of the big house, its stone walls were covered with clinging ivy, brown in winter.

Cal opened a door, and we stepped into one of the small dressing rooms. It was decorated luxuriously, with gold hooks, spare terry-cloth robes, and full-length mirrors.

"What are we doing here?" I looked at my pale self in the mirror and made a face.

"Patience," Cal teased, and opened another door that led to a bathroom, complete with shower stall and a rack of fluffy white towels. Now I was really confused.

From his pocket Cal took a key ring, selected a key, and opened a small, locked closet. The door swung open to reveal shallow shelves with toiletries and cleaning supplies.

Cal stood back and gently swept his hands around the door frame, and I saw the faint glimmer of sigils tracing its perimeter. He muttered some words that I couldn't understand, and then the shelves swung backward to reveal an opening about five feet high and maybe two feet wide. There was another room behind it.

I raised my eyebrows at Cal. "You guys have a thing for hidden rooms," I said, thinking of his mother's concealed library in the main house.

Cal grinned. "Of course. We're witches," he said, and ducked through the door. I followed, stepping through, then straightening cautiously on the other side.

Cal stood there, expectant. "Help me light candles," he said, "so you can see better."

I glanced around, my magesight immediately adjusting to the darkness, and found myself in a very small room, perhaps seven feet by seven feet. There was one tiny, leaded-glass window set high up on the wall, beneath the unexpectedly high ceiling.

Cal started lighting candles. I was about to say it wasn't necessary, I could see fine, but then I realized he wanted to create an effect. I looked around, and my gaze landed on the burnt wick of a thick cream-colored pillar candle. I need fire, I thought, then blinked as the wick burst into flame.

It mesmerized me, and I leaned, timelost, into the wavering, triangular bloom of flame swaying seductively about the wick. I saw the wick shrivel and curl as the intense heat made the fibers contract and blacken, heard the roar of the victorious fire as it consumed the wick and surged upward in ecstasy. I felt the softening of the wax below as it sighed and acquiesced, melting and flowing into liquid.

My eyes shining, I glanced up to see Cal staring at me almost in alarm. I swallowed, wondering if I had made one of those Wiccan faux pas I was so good at.

"The fire," I murmured lamely in explanation. "It's pretty."

"Light another one," he said, and I turned to the next candle and thought about fire, and an unseen spark of life jumped from me to the wick, where it burst into a bloom of light. He didn't have to encourage me to do more. One by one, I lit the candles that lined the walls, covered the tiny bookcase, dripped out of wine bottles, and guttered on top of plates thick with old wax.

The room was now glowing, the hundreds of small flames lighting our skin, our hair, our eyes. In the middle of the floor was a single futon covered with a thin, soft, oriental rug. I sat on it, clasped my arms around my knees, and looked around me. Cal sat next to me.

"So this is your secret clubhouse?" I asked, and he chuckled and put his arm around me.

"Something like that," he agreed. "This is my sanctuary."

Now that I wasn't lighting candles, I had the time to be awestruck by my surroundings. Every square inch of wall and ceiling was painted with magickal symbols, only some of which I recognized. My brows came together as I tried to make out runes and marks of power.

My mathematician's brain started ticking: Cal and Selene had moved here right before school started—the beginning of September. It was almost the end of November now: that left not quite three months. I turned to look at him.

"How did you do all this in three months?"

He gave a short laugh. "Three months? I did this in three weeks, before school started. Lots of late nights."

"What do you do in here?"

He smiled down at me. "Make magick," he said.

"What about your room?"

"The main house is full of my mother's vibrations, not to mention those of her coven members. My room is fine for most things; it's no problem for us to have circles there. But for my stuff alone, sensitive spells, spells needing a lot of energy, I come here." He looked around, and I wondered if he was remembering all the warm late-summer nights he had been in here, painting, making magick, making the walls vibrate with his energy. Bowls of charred incense littered the floor and the bookshelves, and the books of magick lined up behind them were dark and faded, looking immeasurably old. In one corner was an altar, made of a polished chunk of marble as big as a suitcase. It was draped with a purple velvet cloth and held candles, bowls of incense, Cal's athame, a vase of spidery hothouse orchids, and a Celtic cross.

"This is what I wanted to show you," he said quietly, his arm warm across my back. "I've never shown this to anyone, although my mother knows it's here. I would never let any of the other Cirrus members see this room. It's too private."

My eyes swept across the dense writing, picking out a rune here and there. I had no idea how long we had been sitting there, but I became aware that I was sweating. The room was so small that just the heat of the candles was starting to make it too warm. It occurred to me that the candles were burning oxygen, and Practical Morgan looked for a vent. I couldn't see one, but that didn't mean anything. The room was so chaotic that it was hard to focus on any one thing.

I realized in surprise that I wouldn't be comfortable making magick in this room. To me it was starting to seem claustrophobic, jangling, as if all my nerves were being subtly irritated. I noticed that my breath was coming faster.

"You're my soul mate," Cal whispered. "Only you could handle being here. Someday we'll make magick here, together. We'll surprise everybody."

I didn't know what to think of that. I was starting to feel distinctly ill at ease.

"I think I'd better get home," I said, gathering my feet beneath me. "I don't want to be late."

I knew it sounded lame, and I could sense Cal's slight withdrawal. I felt guilty for not sharing his enthusiasm. But I really needed to get out of there.

"Of course," Cal said, standing and helping me to my

feet. One by one he blew out the candles, and I could hear the minuscule droplets of searing wax splatting against the walls. One candle at a time, the room grew darker, and although I could see perfectly, when the room was dark, it felt unbearable, its weight pressing in on me.

Abruptly, not waiting for Cal, I stepped back through the small door, ducking so I wouldn't whack my head. I didn't stop till I was outside in the blessedly frigid air. I breathed in and out several times, feeling my head clear, seeing my breath puff out like smoke.

Cal followed me a moment later, pulling the pool-house door closed behind him.

"Thank you for showing it to me," I said, sounding stiff and polite.

He led me back to the house. My nerves felt raw as I collected my coat from the front foyer. Outside again, Cal walked me to my car.

"Thanks for coming over," he said, leaning in through the car window.

I was chilled in the frosted air, and my breath puffed out as I remembered the things we had done in his bedroom and the sharp contrast with how I had felt in the pool house.

"I'll talk to you later," I said, tilting my head up to kiss him. Then I was pulling out, my one headlight sweeping across a world seemingly made of ice.

10.
Undercurrents

October 2000

I came home from Ireland this week for Alwyn's initiation. It's hard to believe she's fourteen: she seems both younger, with her knobby knees and tall, coltish prettiness, and somehow also older—the wisdom in her eyes, life's pain etched on her face.

I brought her a russet silk robe from Connemara. She plans to embroider stars and moons around its neck and hem. Uncle Beck has carved her a beautiful wand and pounded in bits of malachite and bloodstone along the handle. I think she'll be pleased when she sees it.

I know my parents would want to be here if they could, as they would have wanted to see my initiation and Linden's. I'm not sure if they're still alive. I can't sense them.

Last year I met Dad's first wife and his other son at one

of the big coven meetings in Scotland. They seemed very Woodbane: cold and hateful toward me. I had wondered if perhaps Dad still kept in touch with Selene—she's very beautiful, very magnetic. But his name seemed to set off a storm within them, which is not unreasonable, after all.

I must go—Alwyn needs help in figuring the positions of the stars on Saturday night.

—Giomanach

That night, after the house was quiet, I lay in bed, thinking. I had been disturbed by Cal's secret room. It had been so intense, so strange. I didn't really like to think about what Cal had done to make the room have those kinds of vibrations, vibrations I could only begin to identify.

And now I knew that Cal was Woodbane. So Hunter had been speaking the truth when he told me that. I understood why Cal and Selene would want to hide it—as Selene said, Woodbanes have a bad reputation in the Wiccan community. But it bothered me that Cal had lied to me. And I couldn't help remembering how he had said that he and Selene were "traditional" Woodbanes. What exactly did that mean?

Sighing, I made a conscious effort to set aside thoughts about my day and immerse myself in Maeve's BOS. Almost every entry in this section was overwritten with an encoded one, and painstakingly I made my way through several days' worth. I already knew that my birth mother had met a witch from Scotland named Ciaran and had fallen in love with him. It was horrible to read about, knowing the whole story of her and Angus. So far it didn't seem like she had slept with Ciaran—but still, the feelings she had for him must have broken Angus's heart. Yet Maeve and Angus had ended up together. And they'd had me.

At last I hid the book and the athame under my mattress. It was the night before Thanksgiving. Hunter's face rose once more before my eyes, and I shuddered. It would be hard, this year, to give thanks.

Downstairs the next morning the kitchen was a crazed flurry: a turkey on the counter, boiling cranberries spitting deep pink flecks of lavalike sauce, Dad—entrusted with only the simplest tasks—busily polishing silver at the kitchen table. Mary K. was wiping the good china, my mother was bustling about, flinging salad, hunting for the packages of rolls, and wondering out loud where she had put her mother's best tablecloth. It was like every other Thanksgiving, comforting and familiar, yet this year I felt something lacking.

I managed to slip outside without anyone noticing. The backyard was serene, a glittering world of icicles and snow, every surface blanketed, every color muted and bleached. What an odd, cold autumn it had been. Kneeling beneath the black oak, I made my own Thanksgiving offering, which I had planned almost a week ago, before the nightmarish events of the weekend. First I sprinkled birdseed on the snow, seeing how the smaller seeds pelted their way through the snow's crust but the large sunflower nuts rested on top. I hung a pinecone smeared with peanut butter from a branch. Then I put an acorn squash, a handful of oats, and a small group of pinecones at the base of the tree.

I closed my eyes and concentrated. Then I quietly recited the Wiccan Rede, which I had learned by heart. I was about to go inside to tell Mom that for some reason, she had left the bags of rolls in the hall closet, when my senses prickled. My eyes popped open, and I looked around.

Our yard is bordered on two sides with woods, a small parklike area that hadn't been developed yet. I saw nothing, but my senses told me someone was near, someone was watching. Using my magesight, I peered into the woods, trying to see beyond the trees.

I feel you. You are there, I thought with certainty, and then I blinked as a flash of darkness and pale, sun-colored hair whirled and disappeared from sight.

Hunter! Adrenaline flowed into my veins and I stood, taking a step toward the woods. Then I realized with a sick pang that it couldn't be him. He was dead, and Cal and I had killed him. It must have been Sky, with that hair. It was Sky, hiding in the woods outside my house, spying on me.

Walking backward, scanning the area around me intently, I moved toward the house and stumbled up the back steps. Sky thought I had killed her cousin. Sky thought Cal was evil and so was I. Sky was planning to hurt me. I slipped into the steamy, fragrant kitchen, soundlessly muttering a spell of protection.

"Morgan!" my mom exclaimed, making me jump. "There you are! I thought you were still in the shower. Have you seen the rolls?"

"Uh—they're in the hall closet," I mumbled, then I picked

up a silver-polishing cloth, sat down next to my dad, and
went to work.

Thanksgiving was the usual: dry turkey, excellent cran-
berry sauce, salty stuffing, a pumpkin pie that was an odd,
pale shade but tasted great, soft, store-bought rolls, everyone talking over each other.

Aunt Eileen brought Paula. Aunt Margaret, Mom and
Eileen's older sister, had finally broken down and started
speaking to Aunt Eileen again, so she and her family joined
us. She spent most of the evening silently but obviously
stewing over the fact that her baby sister was going to roast
in hell because she was gay. Uncle Michael, Margaret's hus-
band, was jovial and good-natured with everyone; my four
little cousins were bored and only wanted to watch TV; and
Mary K. kept making faces at me behind our cousins' backs
and giggling.

All par for the course, I guessed.

By nine o'clock people started trickling homeward.
Sighing, Mary K. plunked down in front of the TV with a
slice of pie. I went upstairs to my room, and I heard Mom
and Dad turn in early and then the click of the TV turning
on in their room.

I turned off my bedroom light, then crept to the window
and looked out. Was Sky still out there, haunting me? I tried
to cast out my senses, but all I got was my own family, their
peaceful patterns in the house. Using my magesight, I looked
deeply past the first line of trees and saw nothing unusual.
Unless Sky had shape-shifted into that small owl on the third
pine from the left, everything was normal.

Why had she been there? What was she planning? My heart felt heavy with dread, thinking about it. I turned my light back on, pulled down my shades, and twitched my curtains into place.

I hadn't talked to Cal all day, and I both wanted to and didn't want to. I longed for him, yet whenever I thought of his secret room, I felt unsettled.

I climbed into bed and took out one of my Wiccan books. I was working my way through about five Wiccan-related books at one time, reading a bit each day. This one was an English history of Wicca, and it was dry going sometimes. It was amazing that this writer had managed to suck the excitement out of the subject, but often he had, and only a determination to learn everything about everything Wiccan kept me going.

I made myself read the history for half an hour, then spent another hour memorizing the correspondences and values of crystals and stones. It was something I could spend years doing, but at least I was making a start.

Finally, my eyes heavy, I had earned the reward of reading Maeve's BOS.

The first section I read described a fight she'd had with her mother. It sounded awful, and it reminded me of the fights I'd had with my parents after I'd found out I was adopted.

Then I found another hidden passage. "September 1981. Oh, Goddess," I read. "Why have you done this? By meeting Ciaran, I have broken a heart that's true. And now my own heart is broken, too.

"Ciaran and I joined our hearts and souls the other

night, on the headland under the moonlight. He told me about the depth of his love for me . . . and then I found out about the depth of his deception, too. Goddess, it's true he loves me more than anything, and I feel in my heart he's my soul mate, my one life love, my second half. We bound ourselves to each other.

"Then he told me another truth. He is already wed, to a girl back in Liathach, and has got two children with her."

Oh, no, I thought, reading it. Oh, Maeve, Maeve.

"Married! I couldn't believe it. He's twenty-two and has been married four years already. They have a four-year-old boy and a three-year-old girl. He told me he'd been forced to marry the girl to unite their two covens, which had been at war. He says he cares for her, but not the way he loves me, and should I give him the word, he would leave her tomorrow, break up his marriage, to be with me.

"But he will never be mine. I would never ask a man to desert his woman and children for me! Nor can I believe that he would even offer. Thank the Goddess, I kept a few of my wits and did not do anything that might see me with my own child by him!

"For this I broke Angus's heart, went against my ma and da, and almost changed the course of my life."

I rested the BOS on my comforter. Maeve's anguished words glowed beneath the blade of the athame, and I felt her pain almost as keenly as if it were my own. It was my own, in a way. It was part of my history; it had changed my future and my life.

I turned the page. "I have sent him away," I read. "He will go back to Liathach, to his wife, who is the daughter of their high priestess. Goddess, he was sickened with pain when I sent him away. If I willed it, he would stay. But after a night of talk we saw no clear path: this is the only way. And despite my fury at his betrayal, my heart tonight is weeping blood. I will never love another the way I love Ciaran. With him I could have drunk the world; without him I will be dosing runny-nosed children and curing sheep my whole life. If it were not a sin, I would wish I were dead."

Oh, God, I thought. I pictured Cal and me being split apart and missed him with a sudden urgency. I looked at the clock. Too late to call. It would have to wait till morning.

I hid the athame and the Book of Shadows, which lately was seeming like a Book of Sorrows, turned out the light, and went to sleep.

My last thought before drifting off was something about Sky, but in the morning I couldn't remember what it was.

On Friday morning I was blessedly alone in the house. I showered and dressed, then ate leftover stuffing for breakfast. My parents had gone to see some old friends of my mom's who were in town for the weekend. Bakker had already picked up Mary K. He had looked less than enthusiastic about Mary K.'s plan to hit the mall for some early Christmas shopping.

After they left, I made an effort to sort through my troubled thoughts. Okay, number one: Hunter. Number two: Cal's secret room. Number three: The fact that Cal lied to me about his Woodbane heritage. Number four: Selene being upset that Cal had told me about their being

Woodbane. Number five: Everything Maeve had gone through with Ciaran and my father. Number six: Sky spying on my house yesterday.

When the phone rang, I knew it was Cal.

"Hi," I said.

"Hi." His voice was like a balm, and I wondered why I hadn't wanted to talk to him earlier. "How was your Thanksgiving?"

"Pretty standard," I said. "Except I made an offering to the Goddess."

"We did, too," he said. "We had a circle with about fifteen people, and we did Thanksgiving-type stuff, witch style."

"That sounds nice. Was this your mom's coven?"

"No," said Cal, and I picked up an odd new tone in his voice. "These are some of the same people who have been coming and going for the last couple of weeks. People from all over. They're Woodbane, too."

"Wow, they're all over the place," I exclaimed, and he laughed. "You can't shake a stick around here without hitting a Woodbane," I added, enjoying his amusement.

"Not in my house, at least," Cal agreed. "Which is why I'm calling, actually. Besides just wanting to hear your voice. There are people here who really want to meet you."

"What?"

"These Woodbanes. Kidding aside, pure Woodbanes are few and far between," said Cal. "Often when they find out about others, they look them up, get together with them, exchange stories and spells and recipes and clan lore. Stuff like that."

I realized I was hesitating. "So they want to meet me because I'm Woodbane?"

"Yes. Because you're a very, very powerful pureblood Woodbane," Cal coaxed. "They're dying to meet the untrained, uninitiated Woodbane who can light candles with her eyes and help ease asthma and throw witch fire at people. And who has the Belwicket tools, besides."

Run, witch, run.

"What?" asked Cal. "Did you say something?"

"No," I murmured. My heart kicked up a beat, and I started breathing as if I had just run up a flight of stairs. What was wrong? Glancing around the kitchen, everything looked fine, the same. But a huge, crashing wave of fear had slammed into me and was now engulfing me and making me shake.

"I feel odd," I said faintly, looking around the room.

"What?" said Cal.

"I feel odd," I said, more strongly. Actually, I felt like I was losing my mind.

"Morgan?" Cal sounded concerned. "Are you all right? Is someone there? Should I come over?"

Yes. No. I don't know. "I think I just need to, um, splash water on my face. Listen, can I call you back later?"

"Morgan, these people really want to meet you," he said urgently.

As he spoke, I was sucked under the swell of fear, so that I wanted to crawl under the kitchen table and curl into a ball. Ask him for help, a voice said. Ask Cal to come over. And another voice said, No, don't. That would be a mistake. Hang up the phone. And run.

Cal, I need you, I need you, don't listen to me.

Now I *was* under the kitchen table. "I have to go," I

forced out. "I'll call you later." I was shaking, cold, flooded with so much adrenaline that I could hardly think.

"Morgan! Wait!" said Cal. "These people—"

"Love you," I whispered. "Bye." My trembling thumb clicked the off button, and the phone disconnected. I waited a second and hit talk, then put the phone on the floor. If anyone tried to call now, they'd get a busy signal.

"Oh my God," I muttered, huddled under the table. "What's wrong with me?" I crouched there for a moment, feeling like a freak. Trying to concentrate, I slowly took several deep breaths. For a minute I stayed there, just breathing.

Slowly I began to feel better. I crawled out from under the table, my knees covered with crumbs. Dagda gazed owlishly down at me from his perch on the counter.

"Please do not tell anyone about this," I said to him, standing up. By now I felt almost back to normal physically, though still panicky. Once more I glanced around, saw nothing different, wondered if Sky was putting a spell on me, if someone was *doing* something.

"Dagda," I said shakily, stroking his ears, "your mother is losing her mind." The next thing I knew, I was putting on my coat, grabbing my car keys, and heading outside. I ran.

11.
Link

I've been studying formally since I was four. I was initiated at fourteen. I've taken part in some of the most powerful, dangerous, ancient rites there are. Yet it's very difficult for me to kindle fire with my mind. But Morgan . . .

Mom wants her desperately. (So do I, but for slightly different reasons.) We're ready for her. Our people have been gathering for weeks now. Edwitha of Cair Dal is staying nearby. Thomas from Belting. Alicia Woodwind from Tarth Benga. It's a Woodbane convention, and the house is so full of vibrations and rivulets of magick that it's hard to sleep at night. I've never felt anything like this before. It's incredible.

The war machine is starting to churn. And my Morgan will be the flamethrower.

—Sgàth

Outside of Practical Magick, I parked Das Boot and climbed out, not seeing the Closed sign until I was pushing on the door. Closed! Of course—it was the day after Thanksgiving. Lots of stores were closed. Hot tears sprang to my eyes, and I furiously blinked them back. In childish anger I kicked the front door. "Ow!" I gasped as pain shot through my toes.

Dammit. Where could I go? I felt weird; I needed to be around people. For a moment I considered going to Cal's, but another strange rush of fear and nausea swept over me, and gasping, I leaned my head against Practical Magick's door.

A muffled sound from within made me peer inside the store. It was dark, but I saw a dim light on in the back, and then the shadow moving toward me metamorphosed into David, jingling his keys. I almost cried with relief.

David opened the front door and let me in. He locked the door behind me, and we stood for a moment, looking at each other in the dimness.

"I feel odd," I whispered earnestly, as if this would explain my presence.

David regarded me intently, then began to lead me to the small room behind the orange curtain. "I'm glad to see you," he said. "Let me get you a cup of tea."

Tea sounded fabulous, and I was so, so glad I was there. I felt safe, secure.

David pushed aside the curtain and stepped into the back room. I followed him, saying, "Thanks for let—"

Hunter Niall was sitting there, at the small round table.

I screamed and clapped my hands over my mouth, feeling like my eyes were going to pop out of my head.

He looked startled to see me, too, and we both whirled

to stare at David, who was watching us with a glint of amusement in his hooded eyes. "Morgan, you've met Hunter, haven't you? Hunter Niall, this is Morgan Rowlands. Maybe you two should shake hands."

"You're not dead," I gasped unnecessarily, and then my knees felt weak, just like in mystery novels, and I pulled out a battered metal chair and sank onto it. I couldn't take my eyes off Hunter. He wasn't dead! He was very much alive, though even paler than usual and still bearing scrapes and bruises on his hands and face. I couldn't help looking at his neck, and seeing me, he hooked a finger in his wool scarf and pulled it down enough for me to see the ugly, unhealed wound that I had made by throwing the athame at him.

David was pouring me a steaming mug of tea. "I don't understand," I moaned.

"You understand parts of it," David corrected me. He pulled up another chair and sat down, the three of us clustered around a small, rickety table with a round plywood top. "But you haven't quite got the big picture."

It was all I could do not to groan. I had been hearing about the big picture since I'd first discovered Wicca. I felt I would never be clued in.

I felt a prickle of fear. I disliked and distrusted Hunter. I'd grown to trust David, but now I thought of how he used to disturb me. Could I trust anyone? Was anyone on my side? I looked from one to the other: David, with his fine, short, silver hair and measuring brown eyes; Hunter, his golden hair so like Sky's but with green eyes where hers were black.

"You're wondering what's going on," said David. It was a massive understatement.

"I'm afraid," I said in a shaking voice. "I don't know what to believe."

As soon as I started speaking, it was as if a sand-bagged levee had finally collapsed. My words poured out in a torrent. "I thought Hunter was dead. And . . . I thought I could trust *you*. Everything is upsetting me. I don't know who I am or what I'm doing." Do not cry, I told myself fiercely. Don't you *dare* cry.

"I'm sorry, Morgan," said David. "I know this is very hard for you. I wish it could be easier, but this is the path you're on, and you have to walk it. My path was much easier."

"Why aren't you dead?" I asked Hunter.

"Sorry to disappoint you," he said. His voice was raspier than before. "Luckily my cousin Sky is an athletic girl. She found me and pulled me out of the river."

So Sky had gotten my message. I swallowed. "I never meant to—hurt you that badly," I said. "I just wanted to stop what you were doing. You were killing Cal!"

"I was doing my *job*," Hunter said, his eyes flaring into heat. "I was fighting in self-defense. There was no way Cal would go to the council without my putting a braigh on him."

"You were killing him!" I said again.

"He was trying to kill me!" Hunter said. "And then *you* tried to kill me!"

"I did not! I was trying to stop you!"

David held up his hands. "Hold it. This is going nowhere. You two are both afraid, and being afraid makes you angry, and being angry makes you lash out."

"Thank you, Dr. Laura," I said snippily.

"I'm not afraid of *her*," Hunter said, like a six-year-old, and I wanted to kick him under the table. Now that I knew he was actually alive, I remembered just how unpleasant he was.

"Yes, you are," David said, looking at Hunter. "You're afraid of her potential, of her possible alliances, of her power and the lack of knowledge she has concerning that power. She threw an athame into your neck, and you don't know if she'd do it again."

David turned to me. "And you're afraid that Hunter knows something you don't, that he might hurt you or someone you love, that he might be telling the truth."

He was right. I gulped my tea, my face burning with anger and shame.

"Well, you're both right," said David, drinking from his mug. "You both have valid reasons to fear each other. But you need to get past it. I believe things are going to be very tough around here very soon, and you two need to be united to face them."

"What are you *talking* about?" I asked.

"What would it take for you to trust Hunter?" David asked. "To trust me?"

My mouth opened, then shut again. I thought about it. Then I said, "Everything I know—almost everything—seems to be secondhand knowledge. People *tell* me things. I ask questions, and people answer or don't answer. I've read different books that tell me different things about Wicca, about Woodbanes, about magick."

David looked thoughtful. "What do you trust?"

In a conversation I'd had once with Alyce, she'd said that

in the end, I really had to trust myself. My inner knowledge. Things that just *were*.

"I trust *me*. Most of the time," I added, not wanting to sound arrogant.

"Okay." David sat back, putting his fingertips together. "So you need firsthand information. Well, how do you suggest getting it?"

On my birthday Cal and I had meditated together, joining our minds. Standing, I walked around the table, next to Hunter. I saw the tightening of his muscles, his wariness, his readiness for battle if that was what I offered.

Setting my jaw, focusing my thoughts, I slowly reached out my hand toward Hunter's face. He looked at it guardedly. When I was almost touching him, pale blue sparks leapt from my fingers to his cheek. We all jumped, but I didn't break the contact, and finally I felt his flesh beneath my curled fingertips.

In the street a couple of weeks ago I had brushed past him, and it had been overwhelming: a huge release of emotions so powerful that I had felt ill. It was something like that now, but not as gut-wrenching. I closed my eyes and focused my energy on connecting with Hunter. My senses reached out to touch his, and at first his mind recoiled from me. I waited, barely breathing, and gradually I felt his defenses weaken. His mind opened slightly to let me in.

If he chose to turn on me, I was cooked. Connected like this, I could sense how vulnerable we were to each other. But still I pressed on, feeling Hunter's suspicion, his resistance, and then very slowly his surprise, his acquiescence, his decision to let me in further.

Our thoughts were joined. He saw me and what I knew of my past, and I saw him.

Gìomanach. His name was Gìomanach. I heard it in Gaelic and English at the same time. His name meant Hunter. He really was a member of the High council. He was a Seeker, and he'd been charged to investigate Cal and Selene for possible misuse of magick.

I almost pulled back in pain, but I stayed with Hunter, feeling him searching my mind, examining my motives, weighing my innocence, my connection to Cal. I felt him wonder if Cal and I had been lovers and was embarrassed when he was relieved that we hadn't.

Our breathing was slight and shallow, noiseless in the deep silence of the little room. This connection was deeper still than the one I had forged with Cal. This was bone deep, soul deep, and we seemed to sift through layer upon layer of connection, and suddenly I found myself in the middle of a sunny, grassy field, sitting cross-legged on the ground, with Hunter by my side.

This was nice, and I smiled, felt the sun heat warm my face and hair. Insects buzzed around us, and there was the fresh, sweet smell of clover.

I looked at Hunter, and he at me, and we needed no words. I saw his childhood, saw him with his cousin Athar, who I knew as Sky, felt the agony of his parents' leaving. The depth of his anguish over his brother's death was almost unbearable, though I saw that he had been tried and found not guilty. This was something about which Cal didn't know the truth.

Hunter saw my normal life, the shock of finding out I was a blood witch, the growing sweetness of my love for Cal, the disturbing feelings I'd had about his secret room. I couldn't hide my concern about Mary K. and Bakker, my love for my family, my sorrow over the sadness of my birth mother's life and her unsolved death.

Gradually I realized it was time to go, and I stood up in the field, feeling the grass brush against my bare legs. Hunter and I didn't smile as we said good-bye. We had achieved a new level of trust. He knew I hadn't meant to kill him and that I wasn't part of any larger, darker plan. In Hunter, I had seen pain, anger, even vengefulness, all surrounded by a layer of caution and mistrust—but still, I hadn't seen what I had looked for. I hadn't seen evil.

When I came out of it, I felt light-headed, and David's hand guided me back to my chair. Shyly I glanced up to meet Hunter's eyes.

He looked back at me, seeming as shaken as I was.

"That was interesting," said David, breaking the silence. "Morgan, I didn't know you knew how to join with Hunter's mind, but I suppose I shouldn't be surprised. What did you learn?"

I cleared my throat. "I saw that Hunter wasn't—bad or anything."

Hunter was looking at David. "She ought not to be able to do that," he said in a low voice. "Only witches with years of training—she got right inside my mind—"

David patted his hand. "I know," he said ruefully.

I leaned across the table toward Hunter. "Well, if you're not evil," I said briskly, "why have you and Sky been stalking me? I saw you two in my yard a week ago. You left sigils all over the place. What were they for?"

Hunter twitched in surprise. "They're protection spells," he said.

Just then the back door, a door I had barely noticed, opened. Its short curtain swung in, and a blast of cold air swirled into the room.

"You!" Sky snapped, staring at me from the doorway. She looked quickly at Hunter, as if to make sure I hadn't been trying to kill him in the last twenty minutes. "What is she doing here?" she demanded of David.

"Just visiting," David said with a smile.

Her black eyes narrowed. "You shouldn't be here," she snarled. "You almost killed him!"

"You made me think I *had* killed him!" I snapped back. "You knew what had happened, you knew he was alive, yet you let me think he was dead. I've been sick about it!"

She made a disbelieving face. "Not sick enough."

"What were you doing at my house yesterday? Why were you spying on me?"

"Spying? Don't flatter yourself," she said, flinging down her black backpack. "I've had more important things to do."

My eyes widened. "Liar! I saw you yesterday!"

"No, that was me," Hunter put in, and Sky and I both turned to stare at him.

He shrugged. "Keeping tabs."

His arrogance was infuriating. He might not be evil, but he was still a horrible person.

"How dare you—" I began, but Sky interrupted me.

"Of course he's keeping tabs on you!" she snapped. "He's on the council, and you tried to kill him! If another witch hadn't seen what you'd done and sent me a message to go get Hunter, he would have died!"

I exploded, leaping to my feet. "What other witch? *I* was the one who sent you the message that night! *I* was the one who told you to go get him! And I called 911, too!"

"Don't be ridiculous," Sky said. "You couldn't have sent that message. You're nowhere near strong enough."

"Oh, yes, she is," Hunter said mournfully, leaning his chin on his hand. "She just flushed out my brain. I have no secrets anymore."

Sky gaped at him as if he'd been speaking in tongues. He took careful sips of his tea, not looking at her. "What are you talking about?" Sky asked.

"She did tàth meanma," Hunter said, his accent thickening with the Gaelic words. A shiver went down my spine, and I knew instinctively he'd referred to what we had done, the thing I thought of as the "Vulcan mind meld."

Sky was taken aback. "But she can't do that." She stared at me, and I felt like an animal in a zoo. Abruptly I sat down again.

"You're Athar," I said, remembering. "Athar means Sky. Cousin Athar."

No one had much to say to that.

"She's not in league with Cal and Selene," Hunter offered finally. I got angry again.

"*Cal* and *Selene* aren't in league with Cal and Selene, either!" I said. "For your info, Cal and I have done . . . tàth menama—"

"Meanma," Hunter corrected.

"Whatever. And he wasn't evil, either!"

"Did he lead it or did you?" Hunter asked.

Nonplussed, I thought back. "He did."

"Did you go as deep as with me?" he pressed. "Did you see childhood and future, wake and sleep?"

"I'm not sure," I admitted, trying to think.

"You need to be sure," David told me, almost impatiently.

I looked at all three of them. They seemed to be waiting for my response, and I had nothing to give them. I loved Cal, and he loved me. It was ridiculous to think he might be evil.

A picture of the little room in the pool house suddenly rose in front of my mind's eye. I pushed it angrily away. My mind seized on something else.

"I heard Bree and Raven talking about how you were teaching them about the dark side," I accused Sky.

"Of course I was," she countered, black eyes flashing. "So they could recognize it and fight it! It seems someone should have been teaching you the same thing!"

I stood again, overwhelmed with anger. "Thanks for the tea," I told David. "I'm glad you're not dead," I growled at Hunter. Then I stalked out the back door.

As I stomped down the alley and back to my car, my brain pounded with possibilities. Hunter wasn't dead! It was a huge relief, and waves of thankfulness washed over me. And he wasn't evil! Just—misguided. Unfortunately, Sky was still a total bitch and leading Bree and Raven and the rest of Kithic into what seemed to me to be a gray area.

But first things first. Hunter was alive!

12.
The Bigger Picture

October 2000

Alwyn's initiation went well. I was so proud of her, giving her answers in her clear, high voice. She will grow up Wyndenkell and, we hope, marry within Vinneag, Uncle Beck's coven.

For one moment, as Uncle Beck pressed his athame to her eye and commanded her to step forward, I wondered if her life would be better had she not been born a witch. She would be just a fourteen-year-old girl, giggling with her friends, getting a crush on a boy. As it is, she's spent the last six years memorizing the history of the clans, tables of correspondences, rituals and rites; going to spell-making classes; studying astronomy, astrology, herbs, and a thousand other things along with her regular schoolwork. She's missed school functions and friends' birthdays. And she lost her parents when she was only four.

Is it better for her this way? Would Linden still be alive if he hadn't been a witch? I know our lives would have held less pain if we had been born just human.

But it's pointless to consider. One cannot escape one's destiny—if you hide from it, it will find you. If you deny it, it will kill you. A witch I was born, and my family, too, and witches we'll always be, and give thanks for it.

—Giomanach

When I got home, I found a note saying that Cal had stopped by while I was gone. I ran upstairs, brought the phone into my room, and called Cal's house. He answered right away.

"Morgan! Where have you been? Are you okay?"

"I'm fine," I said, the familiar feeling of warmth coming over me at the sound of his voice. "I don't know what was wrong with me this morning. I just felt so weird."

"I was worried about you. Where did you go?"

"To Practical Magick. And you'll never guess who I saw there."

There was silence on Cal's end, and I felt his sudden alertness. "Who?"

"Hunter Niall," I announced. I pictured Cal's eyes widening, his face showing astonishment. I smiled, wishing I could see him.

"What do you mean?" Cal asked.

"I mean he's alive," I said. "I saw him."

"Where has he been all this time?" Cal asked, sounding almost offended.

"Actually, I didn't ask," I said. "I guess he's been with Sky. She found him that night and brought him home."

"So he wasn't dead," Cal repeated. "He went over that cliff with an athame in his neck, and he wasn't dead."

"No. Aren't you thrilled?" I said. "The weight of this has been so awful. I couldn't believe I had done something so terrible."

"Even though he was killing me," Cal said flatly. "Putting a braigh on me. Trying to take me to the council so they could turn me inside out." I heard the bitterness in his voice.

"No, of course not," I said, taken aback. "I'm glad I stopped him from doing that. We *won* that battle. I don't regret that at all. But I thought I had killed someone, and it was going to be a shadow over my life forever. I'm really, really glad that it won't."

"It's like you've forgotten that he was trying to kill me," Cal said, his tone sharpening. "Do you remember what my wrists looked like afterward? Like hamburger. I'm going to have scars for the rest of my life."

"I know, I know," I said. "I'm sorry. He was—more than wrong. I'm glad I stopped him. But I'm also glad I didn't *kill* him."

"Did you talk to him?"

"Yes." I was getting so weirded out by how Cal sounded that I decided not to tell him about the tàth menima— mamena—whatever. "I also saw his charming cousin, Sky, and we got into an argument. As usual."

Cal laughed without humor, then was quiet. What was he thinking? I felt the need to meld with his mind again, to feel his inner self. But I wanted to lead it myself this time.

That was a disturbing thought. *Did* I have doubts about Cal?

"What are you thinking about?" he asked softly.

"That I want to see you soon," I said. I felt guilty at the partial truth.

"I wanted to see you today," he said. "I asked you, and you said no, and then you went to Practical Magick. You weren't even home when I came by to see if you were all right."

"I'm really sorry," I said. "I just—this morning I felt so strange. I think I was having a panic attack. I wasn't thinking clearly and just wanted to get out of here. But I'm sorry—I didn't mean to blow you off."

"There were people here who wanted to meet you," he said, sounding slightly mollified.

All the hairs on the back of my neck stood up. "I'm sorry," I said again. "I just wasn't up to it today."

He sighed, and I pictured him running a hand through his thick, dark hair. "I've got to do a bunch of stuff tonight, but we've got a circle tomorrow at Ethan's house. So I'll see you there, if not during the day."

"Okay," I said. "Give me a call if you can get away."

"All right. I missed you today. And I'm worried about Hunter. I think he's psycho, and I was relieved when I thought he couldn't hurt either of us anymore."

I felt a sudden twinge of alarm. I hadn't even considered that. I'd have to talk to Hunter and make sure he didn't try to go after Cal again. We'd have to find a way to straighten out all these—misunderstandings or whatever they were— without violence.

"I have to go. I'll see you soon." Cal made a kissing noise into the phone and hung up.

I sat on my bed, musing. When I talked to Cal, I hated the whole idea of Hunter. But today, when Hunter and I were doing the tàth thing, he'd seemed okay.

I sighed. I felt like a weather vane, blowing this way and that, depending on the wind.

After dinner Mary K. and I were in the kitchen, cleaning up. Doing mundane things like working in the kitchen felt a little surreal after my conversation with Cal.

For the hundredth time I thought, Hunter is alive! I was so happy. Not that the world necessarily needed Hunter in it, but now I didn't have his death on my conscience. He was alive, and it felt like a thousand days of sunshine, which was bizarre, considering how I couldn't stand him.

"Any plans for tonight?" I asked Mary K.

"Bakker's picking me up," she answered. "We're going to Jaycee's." She made a face. "Can't you talk to Mom and Dad, Morgan? They still say that I can't go out on dates by myself, I mean, just me and Bakker. We always have to be with other people if it's at night."

"Hmmm," I said, thinking that it was probably a good idea.

"And my curfew! Ten o'clock! Bakker doesn't have to be home till midnight."

"Bakker's almost seventeen," I pointed out. "You're fourteen."

Her brows drew together, and she dropped a handful of silverware into the dishwasher with an angry crash.

"You hate Bakker," she grumbled. "You're not going to help."

Too right, I thought, but I said, "I just don't trust him

after he tried to hurt you. I mean, he held my sister down and made her cry. I can't forget that."

"He's changed," Mary K. insisted.

I didn't say anything. After I'd scraped the last plate, I went up to my room. Twenty minutes later I picked up on Bakker's vibrations, and then the doorbell rang. I sighed, wishing I could protect Mary K. from afar.

Up in my room, I studied my book on the properties of different incenses, essential oils, and brews that one can make from them. After an hour I turned to Maeve's Book of Shadows once more, dreading what I would find out and yet compelled to keep reading. It was so full of sadness right now, of anguish over Ciaran. Even though he had concealed his marriage and proved ready to desert his wife and children, she still felt he was her mùirn beatha dàn. It was hard for me to understand how she could still love him after learning all that. It reminded me of Mary K. and Bakker. If someone had held me down and almost raped me, I knew there was no way I would ever forgive him or take him back.

Who's there? I looked up, my senses telling me that another person's energy was nearby. I scanned the house quickly. I did that so often and was so familiar with my family's patterns that it took only a second to know that my parents were in the living room, Mary K. was gone, and a stranger was in the yard. I flicked off my bedroom light and looked out my window.

I peered down into the darkest shadows behind the rhododendron bushes beneath my window, and my magesight picked out a glint of short, moonlight-colored hair. Hunter.

I ran downstairs and through the kitchen, grabbing my

coat off the hook by the door. Boldly I crunched through the snow across the backyard, then down the side, where my bedroom window was. If I hadn't been looking for him, if I didn't have magesight, I never would have seen Hunter blending with the night's shadows, pressed against our house. Once again I got a strong physical sensation from his presence—an uncomfortable, heightened awareness, as if my system was being flooded with caffeine over and over.

Hands on hips, I said, "What the hell are you doing here?"

"Can you see in the dark?" he asked conversationally.

"Yes, of course. Can't every witch?"

"No," he said, stepping away from the house, dusting off his gloves. "Not every witch has magesight. No uninitiated witch does, except you, I suppose. And not even every full-blood witch has it. It does seem to run strongly in Woodbanes."

"Then you must have it," I said. "Since you're half Woodbane."

"Yes, I do," he said, ignoring the challenge in my voice. "In me it developed when I was about fifteen. I thought it had to do with puberty, like getting a beard."

"What are you doing here?"

"Redrawing the protection sigils on your house," he said, as if he was saying, Just neatening up these bushes. "I see Cal laid his own on top of them."

"He was protecting me from you," I said pointedly. "Who are *you* protecting me from?"

His grin was a flash of light in the darkness. "Him."

"You're not planning to try to bind him again, are you?" I asked. "To put the braigh on him? Because you know I won't let you hurt him."

"No fear, I'm not trying that again," Hunter said. He touched his neck gingerly. "I'm just watching—for now, anyway. Until I get proof of what he's up to. Which I will."

"This is great," I said, disgusted. "I'm tired of both of you. Why don't you two leave me out of whatever big picture you're playing out?"

"I wish I could, Morgan," said Hunter, sounding sober. "But I'm afraid you're part of the picture, whether you want to be or not."

"But why?" I cried, fed up.

"Because of who you are," he said. "Maeve was from Belwicket."

"So?" I rubbed my arms up and down my shoulders, feeling chilled.

"Belwicket was destroyed by a dark wave, people said, right?"

"Yes," I said. "In Maeve's Book of Shadows, she said a dark wave came and wiped out her coven. It killed people and destroyed buildings. My dad went to look at the town. He said there's hardly anything left."

"There isn't," said Hunter. "I've been there. The thing is, Belwicket wasn't the only coven destroyed by this so-called dark wave. I've found evidence of at least eight others, in Scotland, England, Ireland, and Wales. And those are only the ones where it was obvious. This—force, whatever it is—could be responsible for much more damage, on a smaller scale."

"But what is it?" I whispered.

"I don't know," Hunter said, snapping a small branch in frustration. "I've been studying it for two years now, and I still don't know what the hell I'm dealing with. An evil force of some kind. It destroyed my parents' coven and made my parents go into hiding. I haven't seen them in almost eleven years."

"Are they still alive?"

"I don't know." He shrugged. "No one knows. My uncle said they went into hiding to protect me, my brother, my sister. No one's seen them since."

The parallels were clear. "My birth parents went into hiding, here in America," I said. "But they were killed two years later."

Hunter nodded. "I know. I'm sorry. But they're not the only ones who have died. I've counted over a hundred and forty-five deaths in the eight covens I know about."

"And no one knows what it is," I stated.

"Not yet." His frustration was palpable. "But I'll find out. I'll chase it till I know."

For a long minute we stood there, not speaking, each lost in our thoughts.

"What happened with Linden?" I asked.

Hunter flinched as if I'd struck him. "He was also trying to solve the mystery of our parents' disappearance," he said in a low voice. "But he called up a force from the other side, and it killed him."

"I don't understand," I said. A chill breeze riffled my hair, and I shivered. Should I ask Hunter in? Maybe we could hang in the kitchen or family room. It would be warm there.

"You know, a dark spirit," Hunter said. "An evil force. I'm guessing the dark wave is either an incredibly powerful force like that or a group of many of them, banded together."

This was too much for me to take in. "You mean, like a dead person?" My voice squeaked. "A ghost?"

"No. Something that's never been alive."

I shivered again and wrapped my arms around myself. Before I knew it, Hunter was rubbing my back and arms, trying to warm me up. I glanced up at his face in the moonlight, at his carved cheekbones, the green glitter of his eyes. He was beautiful, as beautiful as Cal in his own way.

This is who hurt Cal, I reminded myself. He put a braigh on Cal and hurt him.

I stepped away, no longer wanting to ask him inside. "What will you do with this dark force when you find it?" I asked.

"I won't be able to do anything to it," he said. "What I hope to do is to stop the people who keep calling it into existence."

I stared at him. He held my gaze; I saw him glance at my mouth.

"And then," he said quietly, "maybe then people who have been hurt by this, like you, like me . . . will be able to get on with their lives."

His words fell like quiet leaves onto the snow as I stood, trapped by his eyes. My chest hurt, as if I had too much emotion inside, and to let it all out was unthinkable: I wouldn't know where to begin.

Frozen, I watched Hunter lean closer to me, and then his hand was on my chin, and it was cold, like ice, and he tilted up my face. Oh, Goddess, I thought. He's going to kiss me. Our eyes were locked on each other, and again I felt that connection with him, with his mind, his soul. A small spot of heat at my throat reminded me that I wore Cal's silver pentacle on a cord around my neck. I blinked and heard a car drive up and realized what we were doing, and I stepped back and pushed against him with my hands.

"Stop that!" I said, and he looked at me with an unfathomable expression.

"I didn't mean to," he said.

A car door opened, then slammed shut, then opened, and Mary K.'s voice said, "Bakker!" Her tone was shrill, alarmed.

Before the door slammed shut again, I was running across the yard to find Mary K., with Hunter right behind me.

Bakker had parked in front of our house. Inside the dark car I caught glimpses of arms and legs and the auburn flash of my sister's hair. I yanked the car door open, spilling Mary K. on her back into the snow, her legs up on the car seat.

Hunter reached down to help Mary K. up. Tear tracks were already frosting on my sister's face, and one of her jacket's buttons had been ripped. She was starting to cry and hiccup at the same time. "M-M-Morgan," she stammered.

I leaned into the car to glare at Bakker.

"You stupid bastard," I said in a low, mean voice. I felt cold with rage. If I'd had an athame right then, I would have stabbed him.

"Stay out of it," he said, sounding upset. He had scratch marks on one cheek. "Mary K.!" he called, shifting in his seat as if he would get out. "Come back—we need to talk."

"If you ever look at, touch, talk to, or stand next to my sister again," I said very softly, "I'll make you sorry you were ever born." I didn't feel at all afraid or panicky: I wanted him to get out of the car and come after me so I could rip him apart.

His face turned red with anger. "You don't scare me with all that witch crap," he spat.

An evil smile snaked across my face. "Oh, but I should," I whispered, and watched the color drain from his cheeks. I narrowed my eyes at him for a second, then drew out of the car and slammed the door shut.

Hunter was watching us from a few feet away. Mary K. was holding his arm, and now she blinked up at him, saying, "I know you."

"I'm Hunter," he said as Bakker peeled away, burning rubber.

"Come on, Mary K.," I said, taking her arm and leading her toward the house. I didn't want to look at Hunter—I was still trying to process that almost kiss.

"Are you okay?" I asked, hugging Mary K. to my side as we went up the steps.

"Yes," she said shakily. "Just get me upstairs."

"Will do."

"I'll see you later, Morgan," said Hunter. I didn't reply.

13.
The Circle

Giomanach is alive. Back from the dead. Dammit! Having the council's dog breathing down our necks could ruin everything. I need to take care of him. It's my responsibility.

I'll put the braigh on him, around his neck, and he can see how it feels.

—Sgàth

The next day Mary K. came into the family room as I was researching correspondences on the computer. There were dozens of Wiccan sites on-line, and I loved cruising from one to another.

"Morgan?"

"Yeah? Hey." I turned to look at her. Head hanging down, she looked uncharacteristically drawn and defenseless. I stopped what I was doing and pulled her into a tight hug.

"Why did he do it?" she whispered, her tears making

my cheeks wet. "He says he loves me. Why does he try to hurt me?"

A rage began to boil in me. Was there some kind of spell I could do to Bakker that would teach him a lesson?

"I don't know," I told her. "He can't take no for an answer. Somehow he doesn't mind hurting you."

"He *does* mind," Mary K. cried. "He doesn't want to hurt me. But he always does."

"If he can't control himself, he needs help," I said slowly and carefully. "He needs to be in therapy. He's going to end up killing someone someday, a girlfriend or a wife." I pulled away and looked my sister in the eyes. "And Mary K.? That person will not be you. Understand?"

She looked at me helplessly, her eyes awash with tears. I shook her shoulders gently, once, twice, until she nodded.

"It won't be me," she said.

"It's over this time," I said. "Right?"

"Right," she said, but her eyes slid away, and I swore to myself.

"Do you want to tell Mom and Dad about him, or should I?" I said briskly.

"Oh, uh . . ."

"I'll tell them," I said, setting off to find them. In my opinion, keeping this a secret only made it more likely it would happen again. If my folks knew, Mary K. would have a harder time forgiving Bakker and going back to him again.

My parents did not take it well. They were angry with me for not telling them sooner, furious with Mary K. for continuing to see Bakker after the first time, and almost murderous in their rage toward Bakker, which cheered me up. In the end there was a big group hug, complete with tears and sobbing.

Half an hour later I paced off a small plot in the back-yard, where my parents had agreed I could have a garden. The ground was too hard to dig, but I hammered in stakes and string to show where next spring's herbs would be. Then I sat on the snowy ground and tried to meditate for a while, clearing my mind and sending good thoughts into the earth below me, thanking it for being receptive to my gar-den. Feeling refreshed, I went back inside to look for a spell to put on Bakker.

Technically, of course, I wasn't supposed to do spells. I wasn't initiated, and I'd been a student for barely a couple of months. So I wasn't *committed* to spelling Bakker. But if the necessity arose . . .

Once more we had turkey sandwiches for dinner. I was approaching my saturation point with turkey and was glad to see the carcass was almost bare.

"Any plans for tonight?" my mom asked me.

"Cal's going to pick me up," I said. "Then we're going to Ethan's." Mom nodded, and I could almost see her weighing my boyfriend against Mary K.'s. On the one hand, Cal was Wiccan. On the other hand, he had never hurt me.

By the time Cal rang our doorbell, I had dressed in faded gray cords and the purple batik blouse he had given me for my birthday. I'd French braided my hair to the nape of my neck, then let the rest hang down. In the mirror I looked excited, pink cheeked, almost pretty: a vastly different crea-ture than the Morgan I had been two months ago and a dif-ferent Morgan than just two days ago. Now I knew I wasn't a murderer. I knew I wasn't guilty. I could breathe again, and enjoy life, without Hunter's death hanging over me.

"Hi!" I greeted Cal, shuffling into my coat. I said goodbye to my parents, and we walked down the salt-strewn pathway to the Explorer. In the dark car he leaned over and kissed me, and I welcomed his familiar touch, the faint scent of incense that clung to his jacket, the warmth of his skin.

"How's Mary K.?"

"So-so." I rocked my hand back and forth. I'd told him the gist of what had happened last night, omitting the Hunter part. "I've decided to fix it so that every time Bakker speaks, a toad or snake will slither from his mouth."

Cal laughed and turned onto the main street that would take us to Ethan's. "You are one bloodthirsty woman," he said. Then he flicked me a serious glance. "No spells, okay? Or at least, please talk to me about them first."

"I'll try," I said with exaggerated virtue, and he laughed again.

He parked in back of Robbie's red Beetle outside Ethan's house and turned to me again. "I haven't seen you in days, it feels like." He looped his hand around my neck and pulled me closer for a breathless kiss.

"Just one day," I answered, kissing him back.

"I wanted to ask you—what did you think about my seòmar?"

"What's a shomar?"

"Seòmar," Cal corrected my pronunciation. "It's a private place, usually used by one witch alone, to work magick. Different from a place where you meet with others."

"Does every witch have one?" I asked.

"No. Quit evading the question. What did you think of *mine?*"

"Well, I found it sort of disturbing," I said. I didn't want to hurt his feelings, but I couldn't lie, either. "After a while I wanted to get out of there."

He nodded, then opened the car door and got out. We walked up the pavement to Ethan's small, split-level brick rambler. "That's natural," he said, not sounding offended. "I'm the only one who's worked there, and I've done some intense stuff. I'm not surprised it seemed a little uncomfortable." He sounded relieved. "You'll get used to it pretty fast."

He rang the doorbell while I wondered if I even wanted to get used to it.

"Hey, man," said Ethan. "Come on in."

This was the first time I'd been to Ethan's house: before we were coven mates, we'd never socialized in or out of school. Now I saw that his house was modest but tidy, the furniture worn but cared for. Suddenly two small apricot bundles skittered around the corner from the hall, barking wildly, and I backed up a little.

Jenna laughed from the couch. "Here, pup dogs," she called. The two doglets ran toward her, panting happily, and Jenna gave them each a tortilla chip. She'd obviously been here before and knew Ethan's dogs. Another surprise.

"I never figured you for Pomeranians," Cal told Ethan with a straight face.

"They're my mom's," Ethan said, scooping one under each arm and carrying them back down the hall.

Robbie came out of the kitchen, munching a chip. Matt arrived last, and we went downstairs to the basement, which had been finished to be a large family room.

"Is Sharon still out of town?" I asked, helping Ethan push back furniture.

"Yeah. In Philly," he said. He pushed one of his straggly ringlets out of his eyes.

Once the furniture was out of the way, Cal started unpacking his leather satchel, taking out his Wiccan tools.

"Hey, Jenna," Matt said, since she had ignored him upstairs. His usual pressed appearance had taken a downslide in the last few days: his hair was no longer brushed smooth, his clothes looked less carefully chosen.

Jenna met his gaze squarely, then turned away from him with no expression on her face. Matt flinched. I'd always thought of Jenna as being kind of needy and dependent on Matt, but now I was beginning to suspect that she'd always been the stronger one.

"Last Wednesday, I asked you to choose your correspondences," Cal said as we settled on the floor around him. "Did anyone have any success?"

Jenna nodded. "I think I did," she said, her voice firm.

"Let us have it," said Cal.

"My metal is silver," she said, showing us a silver bracelet on her wrist. "My stone is rose quartz. My season is spring. My sign is Pisces. My rune is Neid." She lifted her hand and drew Neid in the air. "That's all I have."

"That's plenty," said Cal. "Good work. Your rune, standing for delay and the need for patience, is very apt."

He fished in his satchel and took out a squarish chunk of rose quartz the size of an egg. It was pale pink, mostly clear, not milky, and inside were cracks and flaws that looked like broken windowpanes, trapped inside. I thought it looked like pink champagne, frozen in time. Cal handed it to Jenna. "This is for you. You'll use it in your spells."

"Thanks," Jenna said, looking deeply into it, pleased.

"Your rune, Neid, will also become important. For one thing, you can use it as a signature, either on your spells or even in notes and letters."

Jenna nodded.

I sat forward, excited. This was cool stuff—this was what I really loved about Wicca. In my Wicca books the use of quartz in various spells had come up again and again. It had been used religiously for thousands of years. In particular, pink or rose quartz was used to promote love, peace, and healing. Jenna could use all three.

"Robbie?" Cal asked.

"Yeah," he said. "Well, I'm a Taurus, my rune is Eoh, the horse, which also symbolizes travel or change of some kind. My metal is copper. My herb is mugwort. My stone is emerald."

"Interesting." Cal grinned at us. "This is really interesting. You guys are doing a great job of feeling your way to your essences. Robbie, I didn't even associate emerald with you, but as soon as you said it, I thought, yeah, of course." He reached into his bag, rejecting several stones, then brought one out.

"This is a rough emerald," he said, holding it toward Robbie. It was about the size of a pat of butter, a dark, greenish lump in his hand. Robbie took it. "Don't get excited—it's not gem quality. No jeweler would buy it from you. Use it in good health," said Cal, and I was oddly reminded of taking communion at church. Cal went on, "Emerald is good for attracting love and prosperity, to strengthen the memory, to protect its user, and also to improve the eyesight."

Robbie turned and wiggled his eyebrows at me. Until about a month ago, he'd worn thick glasses. My healing potion had had the unexpected side benefit of perfecting his vision.

"So do you just have every stone possible in that bag?" Ethan asked.

Cal grinned. "Not every one. But I have one or two of the most typical."

I had been wondering the same thing myself.

"Okay, Matt?" Cal prompted

Matt swallowed. "I'm a Gemini," he said. "My rune is Jera. My stone is tourmaline."

"Jera, for karma, a cyclical nature, the seasons," said Cal. "Tourmaline."

"The kind with two colors," Matt said.

"They call that watermelon tourmaline," said Cal, and took one out. It looked like a hexagonal piece of quartz, about an inch and a half long and as thick as a pencil. It was green on one end, clear in the middle, and pink on the other end. Cal handed it to Matt, saying, "Wearing this balances the user. Use it in good health."

Matt nodded and turned the stone over in his hand.

"I can go next," said Ethan. "I know what Sharon's are— should I tell them to you?"

Cal shook his head. "She can tell us at the next circle or at school."

"Okay, then, mine," said Ethan. "I'm a Virgo. My season is summer. My stone is brown jasper. I don't have a plant or anything. My favorite jellybean flavor is sour apple."

"Okay," said Cal, smiling. "Good. I think I have a piece of brown jasper . . . hang on." He looked at the stones in his bag and pulled out one that looked like solidified root beer. "Here you go. Brown jasper is especially good for helping you keep your feet on the ground."

Ethan nodded, looking at his stone.

"I think for your rune, you should use . . ." Cal considered Ethan thoughtfully while we all waited. "Beorc. For new beginnings, a rebirth. Sound okay?"

"Yeah," Ethan said. "Beorc. Cool."

Cal turned to me with a special look. "Last but not least?"

"I'm on the Scorpio-Sagittarius cusp," I said. "Mostly Sagittarius. My herb is thyme. My rune is Othel, which stands for an ancestral home, a birthright. My stone is bloodstone."

I might have been the only one to see Cal's pupils dilate and then contract in an instant. Was my choice wrong? Maybe I should have run my ideas by him first, I thought uncertainly. But I had been so sure.

Cal let a stone drop unseen into his bag; I heard it click faintly. "Bloodstone," he said, trying it out. I met his gaze as he looked at me. "Bloodstone," he repeated.

"What are its properties?" Jenna asked.

"It's very old," said Cal. "It's been used in magick for thousands of years to give strength to warriors in battle, to help women through childbirth. They say it can be used to break ties, open doors, even knock down barriers." He paused, then reached into his bag again, rummaged around, and pulled out a large, dark green stone, smooth and polished. When he tilted it this way and that, I could see the dark, blood-colored flecks of red within its darkness.

"Bloodstone," repeated Cal, examining it. "Its ruling planet is Mars, which lends it qualities of strength, healing, protection, sexual energy, and magick involving men."

Jenna grinned at me, and I felt my cheeks flush.

"It's a fire stone," Cal went on, "and its associated color is red. In spells you could use it to increase courage, magickal power, wealth, and strength." His eyes caught mine. "Very interesting." He tossed me the stone, and I caught it. It felt smooth and warm in my hand. I had come across another bloodstone among the things in Maeve's toolbox. Now I had two.

"Okay, now let's make a circle," said Cal, standing. He quickly drew a circle, and we all helped cast it: purifying it, invoking the four elements and the Goddess and God, linking hands within it. Without Sharon there were only six of us. I looked around and realized that I was starting to feel like these people were my second family.

Each of us held our stones in our right palm, sandwiched with the left palm of the person next to us. We moved in our circle, chanting. Looking forward to the rush of ecstatic energy I always got in a circle, I moved around and around, watching everyone's faces. They were intent, focused, perhaps more so than during other circles: their stones must be at work. Jenna looked lovely, ethereal as delight crossed her features. Wonderingly she glanced at me, and I smiled at her, waiting for my own magick to take me away.

It didn't. It was a while before I realized I was deliberately holding it down, not letting it go, not letting myself give in to the magick. It occurred to me: I didn't feel safe. There was no reason I could think of not to, but I simply didn't. My own magick stayed dampened, not the enormous outpouring of power that it usually was. I let out a deep breath and put my trust in the Goddess. If there was danger here that I couldn't see, I hoped she would take care of me.

Gradually Cal took us down, and as we slowed, my coven members looked at me expectantly. They were used to me having to ground myself after a circle, and this time, when I shook my head, they seemed surprised. Cal gave me a questioning look, but I just shrugged.

Then Jenna said, "I feel kind of sick."

"Sit down," Cal said, moving to her side. "Ground yourself. All of you may feel some increased sensations because of your stones and the inner work you did over the week."

Cal helped Jenna sit cross-legged on the carpeted floor, her forehead touching the floor, both hands out flat. He took her chunk of pink quartz and placed it on the back of her slender neck, exposed because her ash blond hair had slipped down on both sides.

"Just breathe," he said gently, keeping one hand on her back. "It's okay. You're just getting in touch with your magick."

Robbie sat down, too, and assumed the same position. This was amazing. The others were finally picking up on the kind of magickal energy I'd been overwhelmed by since the beginning. Forgetting about my own weird feelings, I met Cal's eyes and smiled. Our coven was coming together.

An hour later Cal ended the circle. I stood and got my coat from the hall.

"It was a great circle tonight, guys," Cal said, and everyone nodded enthusiastically. "School starts again Monday,

and we'll all be distracted again, so let's try to keep focused.
I think you'll find it's easier to do now that you have your
working stones. And just remember, we have a rival coven,
Kithic. Kithic is working with witches who are untrustwor-
thy, who have an agenda. For your own sake, I want you all
to stay away from anyone associated with them."

I looked at Cal in surprise. He hadn't mentioned his inten-
tion of telling us this, but I supposed it was only natural, given
the connection between Hunter and Sky, Sky and Kithic.

"We can't just be friends with them?" asked Jenna.

Cal shook his head. "It might not be safe. Everyone, be
careful, and if anything feels strange or you feel things you
can't figure out, please tell me right away."

"You mean like spells?" Ethan asked with a frown. "Like if
they put spells on us?"

"I don't think they will," Cal said quickly, raising his
hands. "I'm just saying be alert and talk to me about everything and anything, no matter how small."

Robbie looked impassively at Cal. I doubted he planned
to quit seeing Bree. Matt looked completely depressed—he
didn't seem to have a choice about seeing Raven or not: she
wanted to see him, and so far he hadn't been able to say no.

Cal and I went out to the car, and I was silent with
thought.

14.
Finding

December 2000

My petition to become a Seeker has gone to the top. Yesterday I met with the seven elders of the council. They once again turned me down. What to do now?

I must curb my anger. Anger cannot help me here. I will ask Uncle Beck to intercede on my behalf. In the meantime I am taking classes with Nera Bluenight, of Calstythe. With her guidance I can school my emotions more and petition the council once again.

—Giomanach

On Sunday morning I realized that one week ago today I had turned seventeen. Looking back, it had been an intensely unhappy day: trying to appear normal while reliving the horror of watching Hunter go over the ledge, the dismay over Cal's wounds, the temporary loss of my magick.

This week was going better. Thank the Goddess and God, Hunter was alive. I felt reassured by knowing that he wasn't inherently evil—and neither was I.

Yet there were still huge, unresolved issues in my life. Questions about Cal and the things he might or might not be hiding from me, questions about myself and the depth of my commitment to Cal, to Wicca itself . . .

I went to church with my family because I knew my mother would make a fuss if I tried to duck out for the second week in a row, and I just wasn't ready to fight that battle. I sleepwalked through the service, my mind churning ideas incessantly. I felt I was two people: Catholic and not Catholic. Part of my family and not part of my family. In love with Cal, yet holding back. Loathing Hunter and yet full of joy that he was alive. My whole life was a mishmash, and I was being divided in two.

When the time for communion approached, I slipped out of our pew as if I was heading for the bathroom. I stood in the drafty hall behind the organist's cubby for a couple of minutes, then came back and fell in line with the people who had just taken communion. I took my seat, dabbing my lips as if I'd just sipped from the chalice. My mother gave me a questioning look but didn't say anything. Leaning back, I let my thoughts drift away once again.

Suddenly Father Hotchkiss's booming voice startled me. From the pulpit he thundered, "Does the answer lie within or without?"

It was like a bolt of lightning. I stared at him.

"For us," Father Hotchkiss went on, gripping the pulpit, "the answer is both. The answers lie within yourselves, as your faith guides you through life, and the answer lies without, in the truth and solace the church offers. Prayer is the key to both. It is through prayer we connect with our Maker, through prayer we reaffirm our belief in God and in ourselves." He paused, and the candles glowing behind him seemed to light the whole nave. "Go home," he went on, "pray thoughtfully to God, and ask him for guidance. In prayer will be your answer."

"Okay," I breathed, and the organ started playing, and we stood to sing a hymn.

After church my family had lunch at the Widow's Diner as usual, then headed home. Up in my room I sat on my bed. It was time to take stock of my life, decide where I was going. I wanted to follow the path of Wicca, but I knew that it wouldn't be easy. It would need more commitment from me than the things I was doing. It had to be woven into the everyday cycles of my life. I needed to start living mindfully in every moment.

Serious Wiccans maintain small altars at home, places to meditate, light candles, or make offerings to the Goddess and God, like the one in Cal's seòmar. I wanted to set one up for myself as soon as possible. Also, I had been meditating a bit, but I needed to set aside time to do it every day.

Making these simple decisions felt good—they would be outward manifestations of my inner connection to Wicca and my witch heritage. Now for another outward manifestation. Quickly I changed into jeans and a sweatshirt. When the coast was clear, I retrieved Maeve's tools from behind the vent and threw my coat over the box.

"I'm going for a drive," I told Mom downstairs.

"Okay, honey," she replied. "Drive carefully."

"Okay." Out in Das Boot, I put my coat on the seat beside me and cranked the engine. A few minutes later I was approaching the edge of town.

Surrounding Widow's Vale are farmlands and woods. As soon as we had gotten our driver's licenses the year before, Bree and Robbie and I had gone on many day trips, exploring the area, looking for swimming holes and places to hang out. I remembered one place not too far out of town, a large, undeveloped tract that had been cleared for lumber back in the 1800s and was now covered with second-growth trees. I headed there, trying to remember the turns and forks, looking for familiar landmarks.

Soon I saw a field I remembered, and I pulled Das Boot over and put on my coat. I left the car on the shoulder of the road, took Maeve's box, and set off across the field and into the woods. When I found the stream I remembered, a sense of elation came over me, and I blessed the Goddess for leading me there.

After following the stream for ten minutes, I came upon a small clearing. Last summer, when we'd found it, it had seemed a magickal place, full of wildflowers and damselflies and birds. Robbie and Bree and I had lain on our backs in the sun, chewing on grass. It had been a golden day, free of worries. Today I had come back to partake of the clearing's magick again.

The snow here was deep—it had never been plowed, of course, and only faint animal tracks disturbed it. With each step I sank in over my ankles. A boulder at the edge of the clearing made a convenient table. I set Maeve's box there and opened it. Cal had said that witches wore robes instead of their everyday clothes during magickal rites because their clothes carried all the jangled, hectic vibrations of their lives. When I had worn Maeve's robe and used her tools a few days ago, I had felt nauseated, confused. It had occurred to me today that perhaps it was because of the clashing vibrations of my life and my magick.

Father Hotchkiss had advised us to pray, to look within for answers before we tackled outside problems. I was going to take his advice. Witch style.

Luckily for me, it was another one of those weird, warm days. The air was full of tiny dripping sounds as snow melted around me. I shucked my coat, sweatshirt, and undershirt.

It might have been warm for late autumn, but still, it wasn't summer. I began to shiver, and quickly pulled Maeve's robe over my head. It fell in folds to midcalf. I untied my boots, took off my jeans, and even my socks.

Miserably I peered down at my bare ankles, my feet buried in the snow. I wondered how long I would have the guts to stick this out.

Then I realized I no longer felt even the tiniest bit cold.

I felt fine.

Cautiously I lifted one foot, it looked pink and happy, as if I had just gotten out of the bath. I touched it. Warm. As I was marveling about this, I felt a focused spot of irritation at my throat. I touched it and found the silver pentacle Cal had given me weeks ago. I was so used to wearing it that I hardly noticed it anymore, but now it felt prickly, irritating, and regretfully I took it off and put it on the boulder with my other things. Ah. Now I was completely comfortable, wearing nothing but my mother's robe.

I wanted suddenly to sing with joy. I was completely alone in the woods, enveloped in the warm, loving embrace of the Goddess. I knew I was on the right path, and the realization was exhilarating.

I set up the four cups of the compass. In one I put snow, then took out a candle. Fire, I thought, *flame,* and the charred wick burst into life. I used that candle to melt the snow into water. It was harder to find earth, but I dug a hole in the snow and then scraped at the frozen ground with my athame. I'd brought incense for air, and of course I used the candle for fire.

I made a circle in the snow with a stick, then invoked the Goddess. Sitting on the snow, as comfortable as an arctic hare, I closed my eyes and let myself sink through layer upon layer of reality. I was safe here; I could feel it. This was a direct communion between me and nature and the life force that exists within everything.

Slowly, gradually, I felt myself joined by other life forces, other spirits. The large oak lent me its strength, the pine, its flexibility. I took purity from snow and curiosity from the wind. The frail sun gave me what warmth it could. I felt a hibernating squirrel's small, slow heartbeat and learned reserve. A fox mother and her kits rested in their den, and from them I took an eager appetite for survival. Birds gave me swiftness and judgment, and the deep, steady thrumming of the earth's own life force filled me with a calm joy and an odd sense of expectation.

I rose to my feet and stretched my bare arms outward.

Once again the ancient song rose in me, and I let my voice fill the clearing as I whirled in a circle of celebration.

Both times before, the Gaelic words had seemed like a call to power, a calling down of power to me. Now I saw that it was also a direct thread that connected me to Maeve, Maeve to Mackenna, Mackenna to her mother, whose name, it came to me, had been Morwen. For who knows how long I whirled in a kaleidoscope of circles, my robe swirling, my hair flying out in back of me, my body filled with the power of a thousand years of witches. I sang, I laughed, and it seemed that I could do it all at once, could dance and sing and think and see so startlingly clearly. Unlike the last time, I felt no unease, no illness, only an exhilarating storm of power and connection.

I am of Belwicket, I thought. I am a Riordan witch. The woods and the snow faded around me, to be replaced by green hills worn smooth by time and weather. A woman strode forward, a woman with a plain, work-lined face. Mackenna. She held out tools, witch's tools, and a young woman wearing a clover crown took them. Maeve. Then Maeve turned and handed them to me, and I saw my hand reaching out to take them. Holding them, I turned again and held them out to a tall, fair girl, whose hazel eyes held excitement, fear, and eagerness. My daughter, the one I would have one day. Her name echoed in my mind: Moira.

My chest swelled with awe. I knew it was time to let the power go. But what to do with it, where to direct this power that could uproot trees and make stones bleed? Should I turn it inward, keep it within myself for a time when

I might need it? My very hands could be instruments of magick; my eyes could be lightning.

No. I knew what to do. Planting my feet in the churned snow beneath me, I flung my arms outward again and came to a stop. "I send this power to you, Goddess!" I cried, my throat hoarse from chanting. "I send it to you in thanks and blessing! May you always send the power for good, like my mother, her mother, her mother before her, and on through the generations. Take this power: it is my gift to you, in thanks for all you have given me."

Suddenly I was in the vortex of a tornado. My breath was pulled from my lungs, so that I gasped and sank to my knees. The wind embraced me, so that I felt crushed within strong arms. And a huge clap of thunder rang in my ears, leaving me shaken and trembling in the silence that followed, my head bowed to the snow, my hair wet with perspiration.

I don't know how long I crouched there, humbled by the power I myself had raised. I had left this morning's Morgan behind, to be replaced by a new, stronger Morgan: a Morgan with a newfound faith and a truly awesome power, gifted by the Goddess herself.

Slowly my breathing steadied, slowly I felt the normal silence of the woods fill my ears. Both drained and at peace, I raised my head to see if the very balance of nature had shifted.

Before me sat Sky Eventide.

15.
Visions

February 2001

They have accepted me at last. I am the council's newest member—and its youngest, the most junior member of the third ring. I'm one of more than a thousand workers for Wiccan law. But my assigned role is that of Seeker, as I requested. I've been given my tools, the braigh and the books, and Kennet Muir has been assigned as my mentor. He and I have spent the past week going over my new duties.

Now I have been given my first task. There is a man in Cornwall who is accused of causing his neighbor's milk cows to sicken and die. I'm going down there today to investigate.

Athar has offered to come with me. I didn't tell her how glad I was of her offer, but I could see that she understood it nonetheless. She is a good friend to me.

—Giomanach.

Sky was perched on a snow-covered log about fifteen feet away from me. Her eyes were almond-shaped pools of black. She looked pale with cold and very still, as if she had been waiting a long time. Kicking in after the fact, my senses picked up on her presence.

She casually brushed off one knee, then clasped her gloved hands together.

"Who are you?" she said conversationally, her English accent as crisp and cool as the snow around us.

"Morgan," I was startled into replying.

"No. Who *are* you?" she repeated. "You're the most powerful witch I've ever seen. You're not some uninitiated student. You're a true power conduit. So who are you, and why are you here? And can you help me and my cousin?"

Suddenly I was chilled. Steam was coming off me in visible waves. My skin was damp and now turning clammy with sweat, and I felt vulnerable, *naked* beneath my robe.

Keeping one eye on Sky, I dismantled my circle swiftly and packed away my tools. Then I sat on the boulder and dressed, trying to act casual, as if getting dressed in front of a relative stranger in the woods was an everyday thing. Sky waited, her gaze focused on me. I folded Maeve's robe and put it back in my box, and then I turned to face Sky again.

"What do you want?" I demanded. "How long have you been spying on me?"

"Long enough to wonder who the hell you are," she said. "Are you really the daughter of Maeve of Belwicket?"

I met her eyes without responding.

"How old are you?"

A harmless question. "I just turned seventeen."

"Who have you been studying with?"

"You know who. Cal."

Her eyes narrowed. "Who else? Who before Cal?"

"No one," I said in surprise. "I only started learning about Wicca three months ago."

"This is impossible," she muttered. "How can you call on the Power? How can you use those tools without being destroyed?"

Suddenly I wanted to answer her, wanted to share with her what I had just experienced. "I just—the Power just comes to me. It *wants* to come to me. And the tools . . . are mine. They're for me to use. They *want* me to use them. They beckon me."

Sky sighed.

"Who are *you?*" I asked, thinking it was time she answered some questions herself. "I know you're Sky Eventide, you're from England, you're Hunter's cousin, and he calls you Athar." I thought back to what I had learned during the tàth thing with Hunter. "You grew up together."

"Yes."

"What are you doing with Bree and Raven?" I demanded.

After a pause she said, "I don't trust you. I don't want to tell you things only to have you tell Cal and his mother."

I crossed my arms over my chest. "Why are you even here? How did you know where to find me? Why do you and Hunter keep spying on me?"

Conflicting emotions crossed Sky's face.

"I felt a big power draw," she said. "I came to see what it was. I was in my car, heading north, and suddenly I felt it."

"I don't trust you, either," I said flatly.

We looked at each other for long minutes, there in the woods. Sometimes I heard clumps of snow falling off branches or heard the quick flap of a bird's wings. But we were in our own private world, Sky and I, and I knew that whatever happened here would have far-reaching consequences.

"I'm teaching Bree, Raven, Thalia, and the others basic Wiccan tenets," Sky said stiffly. "If I've told them about the dark side, it was only for their protection."

"Why are you in America?"

She sighed again. "Hunter had to come here on council business. He told you he's been doing research about the dark wave, right? He's combining his research with his duties as a Seeker. I get worried about him—all our family does. He's treading on dangerous ground, and we didn't want something bad to happen to him. So I offered to keep him company."

Remembering what Hunter's council duties were, I felt my fists clench. "Why is he investigating Cal and Selene?"

Sky regarded me evenly. "The council suspects they've been misusing their powers."

"In what way?" I cried.

Her dark eyes gazed deeply into mine. "I can't tell you," she whispered. "Hunter believes you're not knowingly involved with their plan. He saw that when you two were in tàth meanma. But I'm not so sure. Maybe you're so powerful that you can hide your mind from others."

"You can't believe that," I said.

"I don't know what to believe. I do know that I don't trust Cal and Selene, and I fear they're capable of more evil than you can imagine."

"Okay, you're pissing me off," I said.

"You need to face the facts. So we need to figure out the facts first. Hunter thinks Selene has a big plan that you're a key element of. What do you think they'll do to you if you don't want to be part of it?"

"Nothing. Cal loves me."

"Maybe he does," Sky said. "But he loves living more. And Selene would stop at nothing to have you—not even her own son."

I shook my head. "You're crazy."

"What does your heart tell you?" she asked softly. "What does your mind tell you?"

"That Cal loves me and accepts me and has made me happy," I said. "That I love him and would never help you hurt him."

She nodded thoughtfully. "I wish you could scry," she said. "If you could see them . . ."

"Scry?" I repeated.

"Yes. It's a somewhat precarious method of divination," Sky explained.

I nodded impatiently. "I know what it is. I scry with fire."

Her eyes opened so wide, I could see the whites around her black irises.

"You don't."

I just looked at her.

Disbelieving, she said, "Not with fire."

Not answering, I shrugged.

"Have you scryed to see what's happening in the present?"

I shook my head. "I just let the images come. It seems to be mostly the past, and sometimes I see possible futures."

"You can guide scrying, you know. You focus your energy

on what you want to see. With water you'll see whatever your mind wants to see. A stone is the best, most accurate, but it offers less information. Do you think you could control scrying with fire?"

"I don't know," I said slowly, my mind already leaping with possibilities.

Ten minutes later I found myself in a situation I never could have dreamed up. Sky and I sat cross-legged, our knees touching, our hands on each other's shoulders. A small fire burned on a flat stone I had unearthed in the snow. It crackled and spat as the snow in the cracks of the burning branches boiled. I'd lit it with my mind, and had felt a stealthy surge of pride at the way Sky's eyes widened in shock.

Our foreheads touched; our faces were turned to the fire. I took a deep breath, closed my eyes, and let myself drift into meditation. I tuned out the fact that my jeans were getting wet and my butt would probably never thaw again. I had never scryed while doing the Vulcan mind meld, but I was into trying it.

Gradually my breathing deepened and slowed, and sometime later I sensed that Sky and I were breathing in unison. Without opening my eyes I reached out to touch her mind, finding the same suspicious brick wall that I had with Hunter. I pushed against it, and I felt her reluctance and then her slow acceptance. Cautiously she let me into her mind, and I went slowly, ready to pull out if this was a trap, if she tried to attack. She was feeling the same fear, and we paused instinctively until we both decided to let down our guards.

It wasn't easy. She had always rubbed me the wrong way, and she just about hated me. Surprisingly, it hurt to see the depth of her dislike for me, the rage she felt over what I had done to Hunter, her suspicion of my powers and their possible sources. I didn't realize witches could transfer their powers to another until I saw her worry that Selene had done this to me.

We breathed together, locked in a mental embrace, looking deeply into each other. She loved Hunter dearly and was very afraid for his safety. She missed England and her mother and father terribly. In her mind I saw Alwyn, Hunter's younger sister, who looked nothing like him. I saw her memory of Linden, how beautiful he had been, how tragic his death was.

Sky was in love with Raven.

What? I followed that elusive thought, and then it was there, in the forefront, clear and complete. Sky was in love with Raven. Through Sky's eyes I saw Raven's humor, her strength, her gutsiness, her determination to study Wicca. I felt Sky's frustration and jealousy as Raven chased Matt and flirted with others and had no reaction to Sky's tentative overtures. To Sky, slender, blond, restrained English Sky, Raven was almost unbearably lush and sexy. The bold way she spoke, her vivid appearance, her brash attitude all fascinated Sky, and Sky wanted her with a frank desire that took me aback and almost embarrassed me.

Then Sky was leading me, asking questions about Cal. Together we saw my love for him, my humiliating relief that someone finally wanted me, my awe at his beauty and respect for his power. She saw my uncertainty about and fascination with Selene and my discomfort about Cal's seòmar. As Hunter had, she saw that Cal and I hadn't made love yet. She saw that Hunter had almost kissed me, and she nearly broke off contact in surprise. I felt like she was paging through my private diary and began to wish I'd never agreed to this. My mind told Sky I had been shocked to find out I was Woodbane and extra shocked just four days ago to learn Cal was Woodbane also.

Now, together, she thought, and I opened my eyes. After looking at each other for a moment, weighing what we had learned, we turned, staying connected, and looked into the fire.

Fire, element of life, Sky thought, and I heard her. Help us see Cal Blaire and Selene Belltower as they are, not as they show themselves to us.

Are you ready to see? I heard the fire whisper back to us seductively. Are you ready, little ones?

We are ready, I thought, swallowing hard.

We are ready, Sky echoed.

Then, as it had for me in the past, the fire created images that drew us in. I felt Sky's awe and joy: she had never scryed with fire before. She strengthened her mind and concentrated on seeing the here and now, seeing Cal and Selene. I followed her example and focused on that also.

Cal, I thought. Selene. Where are you?

An image of Cal's huge stone house formed within the flames. I remembered how I could never project my senses through its walls and wondered if that applied to scrying. It didn't. The next time I blinked, I found myself in Selene's circle room, the huge parlor where she regularly held her coven's circles. It had once been a ballroom and now seemed like a grand hall of magick. Selene was there, in her yellow witch's robe, and I recognized Cal's dark head standing out from a group of people I didn't recognize.

"Do we really need her?" a tall, gray-haired woman with almost colorless eyes asked.

"She's too powerful to let go," said Selene.

An icy trickle down my back told me they were speaking of me.

"She's from Belwicket," a slender man pointed out.

"Belwicket is gone," Selene said. "She'll be from anywhere we want her to be."

Oh, God, I thought.

"Why haven't you brought her to us?" asked the gray-haired woman.

Selene and Cal met eyes, and to me it felt like they fought a silent battle.

"She'll come," said Cal in a strong voice, and inside me I felt a piercing pain, as if my heart were being rent. "But you don't understand—"

"We understand that it's past time for action," another woman said. "We need this girl on our side now, and we need to move on Harnach before Yule. You had an assignment, Sgàth. Are you saying you can't bring her to us?"

"It will be done," said Selene in a voice like marble. Again her gaze seared Cal, and his jaw set. He gave an abrupt nod and left the room, graceful in his heavy white linen robe.

I can't see anymore, I thought, and then I said the words aloud. "I can't see anymore."

I felt Sky pulling back as I did, and I shut my eyes and deliberately came back to the snowy woods and this moment. Opening my eyes, I looked up to see that the sky was darkening with late afternoon, that my jeans were soaked through and miserably uncomfortable, that the trees that had made a circle of protection around me now seemed black and threatening.

Sky's hands slid off my shoulders. "I've never done that," she said in a voice just above a whisper. "I've never been good at scrying. It's—awful."

"Yes," I said. I looked into her black eyes, reliving what I had just seen, hearing Selene's words again. Shakily I uncoiled and stood, my leg muscles cramped, my butt beyond feeling, and an unsettling feeling of nausea in my stomach. As Sky stood, stretching and groaning under her breath, I knelt and scooped up some clean snow, putting it in my mouth. I let it melt and swallowed the cold trickle of water. I did this again, then rubbed snow on my forehead and on the back of my neck under my hair. My breath was shallow, and I felt shaky, flooded with fear.

"Feel ill?" Sky asked, and I nodded, eating more snow.

I stayed on all fours, melting small mouthfuls of snow while my brain worked furiously, trying to process what we had seen. When Bree and I had fought over Cal and I had realized that we were no longer friends after eleven years, it had been shockingly painful. The sense of betrayal, of loss, of vulnerability had been almost unbearable. Compared to what I was feeling now, it had been a walk in the park. Inside, my mind screamed, No, no, no!

"Were those images true?" I choked out.

"I think so," Sky said, sounding troubled. "You heard them mention Harnach? That's the name of a Scottish coven.

The council sent Hunter here to investigate evidence that Selene is part of a Woodbane conspiracy that's trying, basically, to destroy non-Woodbane covens."

"She's not the dark wave?" I cried. "Did she destroy Belwicket?"

Sky shrugged. "They don't see how she could have. But she's been linked to other disasters, other deaths," she said, hammering my soul with each word. "She's been moving around all her life, finding new Woodbanes wherever she goes. She makes new covens and ferrets out blood witches. When the coven is solid, she breaks it up, destroying the non-Woodbane witches and taking the Woodbanes with her."

"Oh my God," I breathed. "She's killed people?"

"They believe so," Sky said.

"Cal?" I said brokenly.

"He's been helping her since he was initiated."

This was all too much for me to take in. I felt frantic. "I have to go," I said, looking around for my tools. It was now almost dark. I grabbed Maeve's box and shook some of the snow off my boots.

"Morgan—" Sky began.

"I have to go," I said, more strongly.

"Morgan?" she called as I took the first step into the woods. I turned back to look at her, standing alone in the clearing. "Be careful," she said. "Call me or Hunter if you need help."

Nodding, I turned again and made my way back to my car. Inside, my heart began screaming again: No, no, no . . .

16. Truth

I've always wondered if my mother killed my father. After all, he left her, not the other way around. And then he had two more kids right away with Fiona. That really freaked Mom out.

Dad "disappeared" when I was almost nine. Not that I'd seen anything of him before that. I was the forgotten son, the one who didn't matter.

When Mom got the phone call, she just told me that Dad and Fiona had vanished. She didn't say anything about them being dead. But as the years have worn on and no one's heard from him—that I know about, anyway—it seems safe to assume he's dead. Which is convenient, in a way. It means Giomanach doesn't have Dad's power behind him. But still, I wish I knew what really happened. . . .

—Sgàth

The sun had faded away. My wheels crunched ice on the road as I drove past old farms, fields of winter wheat, silos.

Cal and Selene. Selene was evil. It sounded melodramatic, but what else do you call a witch who works on the dark side? Evil. Woodbane.

No! I told myself. I'm Woodbane. I'm not evil. Belwicket wasn't evil; my mother wasn't. My grandmother wasn't. But somewhere along the line, my ancestors had been. Was that why Selene wanted me? Did she see the potential for evil in me? I remembered the vision I'd had of myself as a gnarled crone, hungry for power. Was that my true future?

I choked back a sob. Oh, Cal, I screamed silently. You betrayed me. I loved you, and you were just playing a *part.*

I couldn't get over this. It was a physical pain inside me, an anguish so devastating that I couldn't think straight. Tears rolled down my cheeks, leaving hot tracks and tasting of salt when they touched the edges of my lips. A thousand images of Cal bombarded my brain: Cal leaning down to kiss me, Cal with his shirt open, Cal laughing, teasing me, offering to help me with Bakker, making me tea, holding me tight, kissing me hard, harder.

I was flying apart inside. I began to pray desperately that the scrying had been a lie, that Sky had tricked me, made me see things that weren't there, she had lied, had lied. . . .

I needed to see him. I needed to find out the truth. I'd had my questions answered by Hunter and by Sky, and now only Cal remained to fill me in on the big picture, the dangers I was blundering into, the reasons I needed to be careful, to watch myself, to rein in my power.

But first—I had to hide my mother's tools. With all my heart, I hoped that Cal would convince me of his innocence, convince me that Sky was wrong, convince me that our love was true. But the mathematician in me insisted that nothing is one hundred percent certain. I had bound my mother's tools to me, they were mine, and now I had to make sure no one would take them away or make me use them for evil.

But where to stash them? I couldn't go home. I was already almost late for dinner, and if I went home, I wouldn't be able to turn around and leave. Where?

Of course. Quickly I made a right turn, heading to Bree's house. Bree and I were enemies: no one would suspect I would hide something precious in her yard.

Bree's house looked large, immaculately kept, and dark. Good—no one was home. I popped the trunk on my car and took out the box. Whispering, "I am invisible, you see me not, I am but a shadow," I slunk up the side yard, then quickly ducked beneath the huge lilac bush that grew outside the dining-room window. It was mostly bare this time of year, but it still hid the opening to the crawl space beneath Bree's house. I tucked the toolbox out of sight behind a piling, traced some fast runes of secrecy, and stood up.

I was opening my car door when Bree and Robbie drove up in Bree's BMW. They pulled up beside me and stopped.

Ignoring them, I started to swing into the driver's seat of my car. The passenger window scrolled down smoothly. Crap, I thought.

"Morgan?" said Robbie. "We've been looking for you. We were talking to Sky. You've got to—"

"Gotta go," I said, climbing in and slamming the door shut before he could say anything else. I had already talked to Sky, and I knew what she'd said.

Robbie opened his door and started toward me. I peeled off, watching him get smaller in the rearview mirror. I'm sorry, Robbie, I thought. I'll talk to you later.

On the way toward the river, thoughts of exactly what I would say to Cal raced through my mind. I was in the middle of my ninth hysterical scenario when—

Morgan.

My head whipped around. Cal's voice was there, right beside me, and I almost screamed.

Morgan?

Where are you? my mind answered frantically.

I need to see you. Please, right away. I'm at the old cemetery, where we had our circle on Samhain. Please come.

What to do? What to think? Had everything he'd told me been a lie? Or could he explain it all?

Morgan? Please. I need you. I need your help.

Just like that night with Hunter, I thought. Was he in trouble? Hurt? Blinking, I wiped away some stray tears with the back of my sleeve and peered through the windshield. At the next intersection I turned right instead of left, and then I was on the road leading north, out of town. Oh, Cal, I thought, a new wave of anguish sweeping over me. Cal, we have to have it out.

Five minutes later I turned down a side road and parked in front of the small Methodist church that had once shepherded the people who now lay in its graveyard.

Shuddering with leftover sobs, I sat in my car. Then I felt Cal, coming closer. He tapped gently on my window. I opened the door and got out.

"You got my message?" he said. I nodded. He examined

my face more closely. Then he caught my chin in his hands and said, "What's wrong? Why were you crying? Where were you? I tried going by your house."

What should I say?

"Cal, is Selene trying to hurt me?" I asked, my words like shards of ice in the night air.

Everything in him became still, centered, and focused. "Why would you say that?"

I felt his senses reaching out to me, and quickly I shut myself down, refusing him entrance.

"Is Selene part of an all-Woodbane coven that wants to erase non-Woodbanes?" I asked, pushing my hair out of my face. Please tell me it's a lie. Please convince me. Tell me anything.

Cal gripped my hair in his hand, making me look at him. "Who have you been talking to?" he demanded. "Dammit, has that bastard Hunter been—"

"I scryed," I said. "I saw you with Selene and other people. I heard them talking about your 'assignment.' Was I your assignment?"

He was silent for a long time. "Morgan, I can't believe this," he said at last. "You know you can't believe stuff you see in scrying—it's all nebulous, uncertain. Scrying shows you only possibilities. See, this is why I always want you to wait until I guide you. Things can be misunderstood—"

"Scrying showed me the possibility of where my mother's tools were," I said, my voice stronger. "It's not always lies—otherwise no one would use it."

"Morgan, what's this all about?" he asked in a loving voice. He gently pulled me to him so that my cheek rested against his chest, and it felt wonderful and I wanted to sink into him. He kissed my forehead. "Why are you having doubts? You know we're mùirn beatha dàns. We belong together; we're one. Tell me what's wrong," he said soothingly.

With those words the pain in my chest intensified, and I took deep breaths so I wouldn't cry again. "We're not," I whispered, as the truth broke over me like a terrible dawn. "We're not."

"Not what?"

I tilted back my head to look into his gold eyes, his eyes full of love and longing and fear. I couldn't bring myself to say it outright.

"I know you slept with Bree," I lied instead. "I *know* it."

Cal looked at me. Before Bree and I had broken our friendship, she had been chasing Cal hard, and I knew from past experience that she always got whatever guy she wanted. One day she had been happy, saying she and Cal had finally gone to bed, so now they were going out. But they hadn't started going out, and he had come after me. I'd asked him about it before, and he had denied sleeping with her, with my best friend. Now I needed to know the truth of it, once and for all, even as I was being hit with other painful truths from every direction.

"Just once," Cal said after a pause, and inside, I felt my heart cease its pumping and slowly clog shut with ice.

"You know what Bree's like," he went on. "She won't take no for an answer. One night, before I really knew you, she jumped on me, and I let her. To me it was no big deal, but I guess she was hurt that I didn't want more."

I was silent, my eyes locked on his, seeing in their reflection all my dreams exploding, all my hopes for our future, all shattering like glass.

"The only powers she had were reflections coming from you," he said, the barest trace of disdain in his voice. "Once I realized you were the one, Bree was just . . . unimportant."

"Realized I was the one what?" My voice sounded tight, raspy, and I coughed and spoke again. "The one Woodbane around? The Woodbane princess of Belwicket?" I pushed him away. "Why do you keep lying to me?" I cried in anguish. "Why can't you just tell me who you are and what you want?" I was practically screaming, and Cal winced and held up his hands.

"You don't love me," I accused him, still pathetically hoping he would prove me wrong. "I could be *anyone,* young or old, pretty or ugly, smart or stupid, as long as I was *Woodbane.*"

Cal flinched and shook his head. "That isn't true, Morgan," he said, a note of desperation in his voice. "That isn't true at all."

"Then what *is* true?" I asked. "Is anything you've told me true?"

"Yes!" he said strongly, raising his head. "It's true that I love you!"

I managed a credible snort.

"Morgan," he began, then stopped, looking at the ground. His hands on his hips, he went on. "This is the truth. You're right. I was supposed to find a Woodbane, and I did."

I almost gasped with pain.

"I was supposed to get close to her, and I did."

How could I still be standing, I wondered in a daze.

"I was supposed to make her love me," he said quietly. "And I did."

Oh, Goddess, oh, Goddess, oh, Goddess.

He raised his head and looked at me, my eyes huge and horrified.

"And you were the Woodbane, and you didn't even know it. And then you turned out to be from the Belwicket line, and it was like we'd hit gold. You were the one."

Oh, Goddess, help me. Help me, please, I beg you.

"So I got close to you and made you love me, right?"

I had no answer. My throat was closed.

Cal gave a laugh laced with bitterness. "The thing is," he said, "no one said I had to love you back. No one expected me to, including me. But I do, Morgan. No one said I had to fall for you, but I did. No one said I had to desire you, enjoy your company, admire you, take pride in your strength, but I do, dammit! I do." His voice had been rising, and he stepped closer to me. "Morgan, however it started, it isn't like that now. I feel like I've always loved you, always known you, always wanted a future with you." He put his hand on my shoulder, gently kneading and squeezing, and I tried to back up. "You're my mùirn beatha dàn," he said softly. "I love you. I want you. I want us to be together."

"What about Selene?" My voice sounded like a croak.

"Selene has her own plans, but they don't have to include us," he said, stepping closer still. "You have to understand how hard it is to be her son, her only son. She depends on me—I'm the heir to the throne. But I can have my own life, too, with you, and it doesn't have to include her. It's just— first I have to help her finish some things she's been working on. If you help us, too, it will all go so much faster. And then we can be free of her."

I looked at him, feeling a cold, deadly calm replacing the panic and wretchedness inside me. I knew what I had seen in my vision, and I knew Cal was either lying or kidding himself about Selene's plans. They didn't include letting him—or me—be free.

"I'm free of her now," I said. "I know that Selene needs me for something. She's counting on you to sign me up. But I'm not going to, Cal. I'm not going to be part of it."

His expression looked like he had just watched me get hit by a car.

"Morgan," he choked out, "you don't understand. Remember our future, our plans, our little apartment. Remember? Please just help us with this one thing, and then we can work out all the details later. Trust me on this. Please."

My heart was bleeding. I said, "No. Selene can't have me. I won't do what she wants. I won't go with you. It's all over, Cal. I'm leaving the coven. And I'm leaving you."

His head snapped up as if I had hit him, and he stared at me. "You don't know what you're saying."

"I do," I said, trying to make my voice strong, though I really wanted only to crumple in misery on the ground. "It's over. I won't be with you anymore." Each word scarred my throat, etching its pain in acid.

"But you love me!"

I looked at him, unable to deny it even after all this.

"I love *you,*" he said. "Please, Morgan. Don't—don't force my hand. Just come with me, let Selene explain everything herself. She can make you understand better than I can."

"No."

"Morgan! I'm asking you, if you love me, come with me

now. You don't have to do anything you don't want to. Just come and tell Selene herself that you won't be part of her coven. That's all you need to do. Just tell her to her face. I'll back you up."

"You tell her."

His eyes narrowed with anger, then it was gone. "Don't be unreasonable. Please don't make me do anything I don't want to do."

Fear shot through me. "What are you talking about?"

His face had a strange look, a look of desperation. I was suddenly terrified. The next second I whirled, broke into a run, and was digging my car keys out of my pocket. I ripped open the car door, hearing Cal right behind me, then he yanked the door open, hard, and shoved me in.

"Ow!" I cried as my head hit the door frame.

"Get in!" he roared, pushing against me. "Get in!"

Goddess, help me, I prayed as I scrambled to let myself out the other side. But when I grabbed the door handle, Cal put his hand on my neck and squeezed, muttering words that I didn't understand, words that sounded ancient and dark and ugly.

I tried to counter with my Gaelic chant, but my tongue froze in my mouth and a paralyzing numbness swept over me. I couldn't move, couldn't look away from him, couldn't scream. He had put a binding spell on me. Again.

I'm so stupid, I thought ridiculously as he started Das Boot with my keys.

17.
The Seòmar

February 2001

I did it. I put a witch under the braigh.

The fellow in Cornwall was mad, there is no question of that. When I came to question him he first tried to evade me, then when he saw that I would not give up, he flew into a frenzy. He gibbered about how he would curse me and my whole family, that he was one of the Cwn Annwyn, the hounds of Hell. He began to shout out a spell and I had to wrestle him to the ground and put the braigh on him. Then he began to weep and plead. He told me how it burned him, and begged me to let him go. At last his eyes rolled back in his head and he lost consciousness.

I put him in the car, and Athar drove us to London. I left him with Kennet Muir. Kennet told me I'd done well; the man might be mad but he also had true power and was therefore dangerous. He said my task was done, and now it was the seven elders' job to determine the man's future.

I left, and then Athar and I went to a pub and got very drunk. Later, she held me while I wept.

—Giomanach

"You just don't get it, do you?" Cal said angrily, taking a corner too fast. I slumped against the car door helplessly. Inside, my mind was whirring like a tornado, a thousand thoughts spinning out of control, but the binding spell he had put on me weighted my limbs as thoroughly as if I were encased in cement.

"Slow down," I managed to whisper.

"Shut up!" he shouted. "I can't believe you're making me do this! I love you! Why can't you listen to me? All I need is for you to come talk to Selene. But no. You can't even do that for me. The one thing I ask you to do, you won't. And now I have to do this. I don't want to do this."

I slanted my eyes sideways and looked at Cal, at his strong profile, his hands gripping Das Boot's steering wheel. This was a nightmare, like other magickal nightmares I'd had before, and soon I would wake up, panting, in my own bed at home. I just needed to wake up. Wake up, I told myself. Wake up. You'll be late for school.

"Morgan," Cal said, his voice calmer. "Just think this through. We've been working with witchcraft for years. You've only been doing it a couple of months. At some point you'll just have to trust us with what we're doing. You're only resisting because you don't understand. If you would calm down and listen to me, it would all make sense."

Since I was in essence deadweight right now, his telling

me to calm down seemed particularly ironic. Cal kept on talking, but my brain drifted away from his monologue. Focus, I thought. Focus. Get it together. Make a plan.

"I thought you would be loyal to me always," Cal said. My eyes were just above the window ledge, and I saw that we were just entering Widow's Vale. Were we going to Cal's house? It was so secluded—once he got me there, I'd never get out. I thought about my parents wondering where I was and wanted to cry. Focus, dammit! Think your way out of this. You're the most powerful witch they've ever seen; surely there must be something you can do. Think!

Cal flew through a red light at the edge of town, and involuntarily I flinched as I heard the squeal of brakes and an angry horn. I realized he hadn't even put my seat belt on me, and in my present helpless state I couldn't do it myself. Fresh, cold fear trickled down my spine when I pictured what would happen to me in an accident.

Think. Focus. Concentrate.

"You should have just trusted me," Cal was saying. "I know so much more than you do. My mother is so much more powerful than you. You're a student—why didn't you just trust me?"

My door was locked. If I could open it, I could maybe tumble out somehow. And get crushed beneath the wheels since I probably couldn't leap out of the way. Could I unroll my window and shout for help? Would anyone in town recognize my car and wonder why I wasn't driving it?

I tried to clench my right hand and saw with dismay that I could barely curl up my first knuckle.

The night of my birthday, when Cal had put the binding

spells on me, I had somehow managed to break free. I had—pushed, with my mind, like tearing through plastic, and then I had been able to move. Could I do that now?

We raced through downtown Widow's Vale, the three stoplights, the lit storefronts, the cars on their way home. I peered up over my window, hoping someone, anyone, would see me. Would Cal get stopped for speeding? I almost cried as a moment later we passed through downtown and were on the less traveled road that led toward Cal's house. Panic threatened to overtake me again, and I stamped it down.

Bree's face floated suddenly into my mind. I seized on it. Bree, Bree, I thought, closing my eyes and concentrating. Bree, I need your help. Cal has me. He's taking me to Selene. Please come help me. Get Hunter, get Sky. I'm in my car. Cal is desperate. He's going to take me to Selene. Bree? Robbie? Hunter, please help, Hunter, Sky, anyone, can you hear me?

Working this hard mentally was exhausting, and my breath was coming in shallow pants.

"You don't understand," Cal went on. "Do you have any idea what they'd do to me if I showed up without you?" He gave a short, barking laugh. "Goddess, what Hunter did to me that night was child's play compared to what they would do." He looked at me then, his eyes glittering eerily. He looked belovedly familiar and yet horribly different. "You don't want them to hurt me, do you? You don't know what they could do to me. . . ."

I closed my eyes again, trying to shut him out. Cal had always been so in control. To see him this way was sickening, and a cold sweat broke out on my forehead. I swallowed and tried to go deep inside myself, deep to where the power was. Bree, please, I'm sorry, I thought. Help. Help me. Save me. Selene is going to kill me.

"Stop that!" Cal suddenly shouted, leaning over and shaking my shoulder hard.

I gasped, opening my eyes. He glared at me in fury.

"Stop that! You don't contact anyone! Anyone! Do you hear me?" His angry voice swelled in the car's interior, filling my ears and making my head hurt. One hand shook me until my teeth rattled, and I clenched my jaws together. I felt the car making big swerves on the road and prayed to the Goddess to protect me.

"Don't you wreck this car," I said, unclenching my lips enough to speak.

Abruptly he let go of me, and I saw the glare of headlights coming at us and then the long, low blare of a truck horn blowing. It swept past us as I drew in a frightened breath.

"Shit!" Cal said, jerking the steering wheel to the right. Another horn blared as a black car screeched to a halt just before ramming my side. I started to shake, slumped against my door, so afraid, I could hardly think.

You, afraid? part of me scoffed. You're the Woodbane princess of Belwicket. You could crush Cal with the power in your little finger. You have the Riordan strength, the Belwicket history. Now, save yourself. Do it!

Okay, I could do this, I told myself. I was a kick-ass power conduit. Letting my eyes float closed again, trying not to think about the chaos raging around me, I let the music come to me, the timeless music that magick sent. *An di allaigh an di aigh,* I thought, hearing the tune come to me as if borne on a breeze across clover-covered hills.

An di allaigh an di ne ullah. Was that my voice, singing in a pure ribbon of glorious sound that only I could hear? My fingers tingled, as if coming awake. *An di ullah be nith rah.* I drew in a deep, shuddering breath, feeling my muscles twitch, my toes curl. I am breaking this binding spell, I thought. I am smashing it. I am tearing it like wet tissue. *Cair di na ulla nith rah, Cair feal ti theo nith rah, An di allaigh an di aigh.*

I was myself. I had done it. I stayed exactly where I was, opening my eyes and gazing around. With a flare of alarm I recognized the tall hedges that surrounded Cal's property. He swung Das Boot into a side road, skidding a bit, and we began to crunch on icy gravel.

Bree, Sky, Hunter, Robbie, anyone, I thought, feeling my radiating power. Alyce, David, any witch, can you hear me?

The side road to Cal's driveway was long, with tall, overhanging trees. It was pitch-black except where moonlight glistened off snow. The dashboard clock said six-thirty. My family was sitting down to eat. At the thought I felt a surge of anger so strong it was hard for me to hide it. I couldn't accept the possibility that I might never see them again, Mom, Dad, Mary K., Dagda. I would escape. I would get out of this. I was very powerful.

"Cal, you're right," I said, making my voice sound weak. I couldn't even feel the effects of the binding spell anymore, and a surge of hope flamed in my chest. "I'm sorry," I said. "I didn't realize how important this was to you. Of course I'll go talk to your mom."

He turned the wheel and paused, reaching out his left hand and pointing it ahead of him. I heard the metallic rumbling of heavy gates, heard them swing on hinges and clunk open with a bang.

Then, as if he had finally heard me, Cal looked over. "What?" He stepped on the gas, and we rolled through the gate. Ahead of me was a dark roofline, and I realized we were in the backyard, and the building in front of me was the little pool house. Where Cal had his seòmar.

"I said, I'm sorry," I repeated. "You're right. You're my mùirn beatha dàn, and I should trust you. I do trust you. I just—felt unsure. Everyone keeps telling me something different, and I got confused. I'm sorry."

Das Boot rolled slowly to a halt, ten feet from the pool house. It was dark, with the car's one headlight shining sadly on the dead brown ivy covering the building.

Cal turned off the engine, leaving the keys in the ignition. He kept his eyes on me, where I leaned awkwardly against the door. It was all I could do to keep my hand from grasping the door handle, popping the door, and running with all my might. What spell could I put on Cal to slow him down? I didn't know any. Suddenly I remembered how his pentacle had burned at my throat when I used Maeve's tools. I'd felt better without it on. Was it spelled? Had I been wearing a spell charm all this time? I wouldn't doubt it at this point.

With agonizingly slow movement, I slipped my right hand down into my pocket and pulled out Cal's pentacle. He hadn't noticed I wasn't wearing it yet, and I let it slip from my fingers to the floor of the car. As soon as it left my hand, my head felt clearer, sharper, and I had more energy. Oh, Goddess, I was right. The pentacle had been spelled all this time.

"What are you saying?" Cal said, and I blinked.

"I'm sorry," I repeated, making my voice a little stronger. "This is all new to me. It's all confusing. But I've been thinking about what you said, and you're right. I should trust you."

His eyes narrowed, and he took hold of my hand. "Come on," he said, opening his door. His grip on my hand was crushing, and I dismissed the possibility that I could slip out suddenly and run. Instead he pulled me out the driver's side door and helped me stand. I pretended to be weaker than I was and leaned against him.

"Oh, Cal," I breathed. "How did we get into such a fight? I don't want to fight with you." I made my voice soft and sweet, the way Bree did when she talked to guys, and I leaned against Cal's chest. Seeing the mixture of hope and suspicion cross his face was painful. Suddenly I pushed hard against him, shoving with every bit of strength in my arms, and he staggered backward. I raised my right hand and shot a spitting, crackling bolt of blue witch fire at him, and this time I didn't hold anything back. It blasted Cal right in the chest, and he cried out and sank to his knees. I was already running, my boots pounding heavily toward the metal gates that were swinging closed.

The next thing I knew my knees had crumpled and I was falling in slow motion to land heavily, facefirst, on the icy gravel. The breath left my lungs in a painful whoosh, and then Cal stood over me, cradling one arm against his chest, his face a mask of rage.

I tried to roll quickly to shoot witch fire again, the only defensive weapon I knew, but he put his boot on my side and pressed down, pinning me to the cold ground. Then he grabbed one of my arms, hauled me to my feet, and squeezed the back of my neck, muttering another spell. I screamed, "Help! Help! Someone help me!" but of course no one came. Then I sagged, a deadweight.

"An di allaigh," I began in a choking voice as Cal hauled me toward the pool house. I knew where we were going, and I absolutely did not want to go there.

"Shut up!" Cal said, shaking me, and he pushed open the changing-room door. Bizarrely, he added, "I know you're upset, but it will all be okay. Everything will be all right soon."

Reaching out, I grasped the door frame, but my limp fingers brushed it harmlessly. I tried to drag my feet, to be an awkward burden, but Cal was furious and afraid, and this fed his strength. Inside we lurched through the powder room, and Cal let me slump to the floor while he unlocked the closet door. I was trying to crawl away when he opened the door to his seòmar, and I felt the darkness come out of it toward me, like a shadow eager to embrace.

Goddess, I thought desperately. Goddess, help me.

Then Cal was dragging me by my feet into his room. With my magesight I saw that it had been cleared of everything, everything I could have used for a weapon, everything I could have used to make magick. It was bare, no furniture, no candles, only thousands and thousands of dark spells written on the walls, the ceiling, the floor. He'd prepared my prison in advance. He'd known this would happen. I wanted to gag.

Panting, Cal dropped my feet. He hovered over me, then narrowed his eyes and grabbed at the neck of my shirt. I tried to pull away, but it was too late.

"You took off my charm," he said, sounding amazed. "You don't love me at all."

"You don't know what love is," I croaked, feeling ill. I

raised my hands over my eyes and clumsily brushed my hair out of the way.

For a moment I thought he was going to kick me, but he didn't, just looked down at me with the devastating face that I had adored.

"You should have trusted me," he said, sweat running down his face, his breathing harsh.

"You shouldn't have lied to me," I countered angrily, trying to sit up.

"Tell me where the tools are," he demanded. "The Belwicket tools."

"Screw you!"

"You tell me! You should never have bound them to you! How arrogant! Now we'll have to rip them away from you, and that will hurt. But first you tell me where they are—I didn't feel them in the car."

I stared at him stonily, trying to rise to my feet.

"Tell me!" he shouted, looming over me.

"Bite me," I offered.

Cal's golden eyes gleamed with hurt and fury, and he shot out his hand at me. A cloudy ball of darkness shot right at me, hitting my head, and I crashed headlong to the floor, sinking into a nightmarish unconsciousness, remembering only his eyes.

18.
Trapped

June 2001

Litha again. It's now fully ten years since my parents disappeared. When they left, I was a boy, concerned only with building a working catapult and playing Behind Enemy Lines with Linden and my friends.

At the time we were living in the Lake District, across Solway Firth from the Isle of Man. For weeks before they left, they were in bad moods, barking at us children and then apologizing, not having the time to help us with our schoolwork. Even Alwyn started coming to me or Linden to help her dress or do her hair. I remember Mum complaining that she felt tired and ill all the time, and none of her usual potions seemed to help. And Dad said his scrying stone had stopped working.

Yes, something was definitely oppressing them. But I'm sure they didn't know what was really coming. If they had, maybe things would have turned out differently.

Or maybe not. Maybe there is no way to fight an evil like
that.

—Giomanach

When I awoke, I had no idea how much time had passed.
My head ached, my face burned and felt scraped from the
gravel, and my knees ached from when I had fallen on them.
But at least I could move my limbs. Whatever spell Cal had
used on me, it wasn't a binding one.

Cautiously, silently, I rolled over, scanning the seòmar. I
was alone. I cast out my senses and felt no one else near.
What time was it? The tiny window set high on one wall
showed no stars, no moon. I crawled up on my hands and
knees, then unfolded myself and stood slowly, feeling a wave
of nausea and pain roll over me.

Crap. As soon as I stood, I felt the weight of the spelled
walls and ceilings pressing in on me. Every square inch of this
tiny room had runes and ancient symbols on it, and without
understanding them, I knew that Cal had worked dark magick here, had called on dark powers, and had been lying to
me ever since the day I met him. I felt incredibly naive.

I had to get out. What if Cal had left only a minute ago?
What if even now he was bringing Selene and the others
back to me? Goddess. This room was full of negative energy,
negative emotions, dark magick. I saw stains on the floor
that had been hidden by the futon the first time I was here. I
knelt and touched them, wondering if they were blood.
What had Cal done here? I felt sick.

Cal had gone to get Selene, and they were going to put

spells on me or hurt me or even kill me to get me to tell them where Maeve's tools were. To get me to join their side, their all-Woodbane clan.

No one knew where I was. I had told Mom I was going for a drive more than six hours ago. No one had seen me meet Cal at the cemetery. I could die here.

The thought galvanized me into action. I got to my feet again, looking up at the window, gauging its height. My best jump was still two feet short of the window ledge. I pulled off my jacket, balled it up, and flung it hard at the window. It bounced off and clumped to the floor.

"Goddess, Goddess," I muttered, crossing to the door. Its edge was almost invisible, a barely seen crack that was impossible to dig my nails into. In the car I had my Swiss Army knife—patting my pockets quickly yielded me nothing. Still I tried, wedging my short nails into its slit and pulling until my nails split and my fingers bled.

Where was Cal? What was taking so long? How long had it been?

Panting, I backed up across the room, then launched myself shoulder first at the small door. The impact made me cry out, and then I slid down to the floor, clutching my shoulder. The door hadn't even shuddered under the blow.

I thought of how my parents had been so devastated when I took up Wicca, how afraid they had been for me after what happened to my birth mother. I saw now that they'd had good cause to worry.

An unwanted sob choked my throat, and I sank to my knees on the wooden floor. The back of my head ached sickeningly. How could I have been so stupid, so blind? Tears

edged from my eyes and coursed down my bruised and dirty
cheeks. Sobs struggled to break free from my chest.

I sat cross-legged on the floor. Slowly, knowing it was
pointless, I drew a small circle around myself, using my
index finger, wetting the floor with my tears and my blood.
Shakily I traced symbols of protection around me: pentacles,
the intersected circles of protection, squares within squares
for orderliness, the angular runic þ for comfort. I drew the
two-horned circle symbol of the Goddess and the circle/half
circle of the God. I did all these things with only the barest
amount of thought, did them by rote, over and over, all
around me on the floor, all around me in the air.

Within moments my breathing calmed, my tears ceased,
my pain eased. I could see more clearly, I could think more
clearly, I was more in control.

Evil pressed in around me. But I was not evil. I needed to
save myself.

I was the Woodbane princess of Belwicket. I had power
beyond imagining.

Closing my eyes, I forced my breathing to calm further,
my heartbeat to slow. Words came to my lips.

"Magick, I am your daughter"
"I am following your path in truth and righteousness.
Protect me from evil. Help me be strong.
Maeve, my mother before me, help me be strong.
Mackenna, my grandmother, help me be strong.
Morwen, who came before her, help me be strong.
Let me open the door. Open the door. Open the door."

I opened my eyes then and gazed before me at the spelled and locked door. I looked at it calmly, imagining it opening before me, seeing myself pass through it to the outside, seeing myself safe and gone from there.

Creak. I blinked at the sound but didn't break my concentration. I was unsure whether I had imagined it, but I kept thinking, Open, open, open, and in the darkness I saw the minuscule crack widen, just a hair.

Elation, as strong as my earlier despair had been, lifted my heart. It was working! I could do this! I could open the door!

Open, open, open, I thought steadily, my focus pure, my intent solid.

I smelled smoke. That fact registered only slightly in my brain as I kept concentrating on opening the door. But I realized that my nose was getting irritated, and I kept blinking. I came out of my trance and saw that the seòmar was becoming hazy, and the scent of fire was strong.

I stood up within my circle, my heart kicking up a beat. Now I could hear the joyful crackling of flames outside, smell the acrid odor of burning ivy, and see the faint, amber light of fire reflected in the high window.

They were burning me alive. Just like my mother.

As my concentration broke, the door clicked shut again.

Panic threatened to drown me. "Help!" I screamed as loud as I could, aiming my voice at the window. "Help! Help! Someone help me!"

From outside, I heard Selene's voice. "Cal! What are you doing?"

"Solving the problem," was his grim response.

"Don't be stupid," Selene snapped. "Get away from there. Where are the tools?"

I thought fast. "Let me out and I'll tell you, I promise!" I shouted.

"She's lying," said another voice. "We don't need her, anyway. This isn't safe—we have to get out of here."

"Cal!" I screamed. "Cal! Help me!"

There was no answer, but I heard muffled voices arguing outside. I strained to hear.

"You promised she would join us," someone said.

"She's just an uneducated girl. What we really need is the tools," said someone else.

"I'll tell you!" I shouted. "They're in the woods! Let me out and I'll take you there!"

"I'm telling you, we have to leave," someone said urgently.

"Cal, stop it!" said Selene, and suddenly the sound of flames was louder, closer.

"Let me out!" I screamed.

"Goddess, what is he doing? Selene!"

"Get back or I'll torch the whole place with all of us in it," said Cal, sounding steely. "I won't let you have her."

"The Seeker will be here any minute," said a man. "There's no way he won't come for this. Selene, your son—"

I heard more arguing, but I was choking now, the smoke stinging my eyes, and then I heard the popping of the wooden rafters up above. I pressed my ear to the wall and listened, but there were no more voices. Had they all just gone away? If I died in the fire, they would never find Maeve's tools. That wasn't true, I realized. They could scry to find them; they could do spells to find them. The simple concealment runes I had traced around the box wouldn't deceive any of them. They wanted me to tell them only to save time. They didn't really need me at all.

I tried once again to open the door with my mind, but I couldn't focus. I kept coughing and my mind was starting to feel foggy. I slumped against the wall in despair.

It had all been for *nothing*: Maeve hiding her tools to keep them safe, coming to me in a vision to tell me where they were, my finding them with Robbie, my learning how to use them. For nothing. Now they would be in Selene's hands, under her control. And maybe the tools were so old that they had been used by the original members of Belwicket— before the clan promised to forsake evil. Maybe the tools would work just as well for evil as they could for good.

Maybe this was all my fault. This was the big picture everyone kept talking about. This was the danger I was blundering into. This was why I needed guidance, a teacher.

"Goddess, forgive me," I muttered, lying belly down on the smooth wooden floor. I pulled my jacket over my head. I was going to die.

I was very tired. It was hard to breathe. I was no longer panicking, no longer full of fear or hysteria. I wondered how Maeve had faced her death by fire, sixteen years before. With each moment that passed, I had more in common with her.

19.
Burn

June 2001

Here's an interesting thing: I went today to Much Bencham, which is the little town in Ireland next to where Ballynigel used to be. No one there wanted to talk to me, and I got the feeling the whole village was anti-witch. Having seen their closest neighbors turn to dust all those years ago, I'm not surprised. But as I was leaving the town square, an old woman caught my eye. She was probably on the dole—making ends almost meet by selling homemade pasties. I bought one, and as I bit into it she said, very quietly, "You're the lad's been asking questions about the town next door." She didn't name Ballynigel, but of course that was what she meant.

"Aye," I said, taking another bite. I waited.

"Odd things," she murmured. "Odd doings in that town, sometimes. Whole town wiped off the face of the earth. It's not natural."

"No," I agreed. "Not natural at all. Did no one survive, then?"

She shook her head, then frowned as if remembering something. "Though that woman last year said as how some did survive. Some escaped, she said."

"Oh?" I said, though inside my heart was pounding. "What woman was this?"

"She were a beauty," said the old woman, thinking back. "Dark and exotic. She had gold eyes, like a tiger. She came here asking about them next door, and someone—I think it was old Collins, at the pub—he told her they were dead, all of them, and she said no, she said that two made it away to America."

"Two people from Ballynigel went to America?" I said, to make certain. "After the disaster, or before?"

"Don't know, do I," said the woman, starting to lose interest. "She just said that two from there had gone to New York years ago, and that's in America, isn't it."

I thanked her and walked away, thinking. Damn me if that tiger woman didn't sound like Dad's first wife, Selene.

So now I am on my way to New York. Is it really possible two witches from Belwicket escaped the disaster? Could they be in New York? I won't rest until I know.

—Giomanach

Dying from smoke inhalation is not the worst way to go, I thought sleepily. It's uncomfortable and gives you a drowning sort of feeling, but it must be better than being shot or actually burned to death or falling off a cliff.

It wouldn't be long now. My head ached; smoke filled my lungs and made me cough. Even lying on the floor, with my head covered by my jacket, I wouldn't last much longer. Was this how it had been for Maeve and Angus?

When I heard the voices calling my name from outside, I figured I was hallucinating. But the voices came again, stronger, and I recognized them.

"Morgan! Morgan! Are you in there? Morgan!"

Oh my God, it sounded like Bree! Bree and Robbie!

Sitting up was a mistake because even a foot above me, the air was heavier. I choked and coughed and sucked in air, and then I screamed, "I'm in here! In the pool house! Help!" A spasm of coughing crushed my chest, and I fell to the floor, gasping.

"Stand back!" Bree shouted from outside. "Get away from the wall!"

Quickly I rolled to the wall farthest away from her voice and lay there, huddled and coughing. My mind dimly registered the familiar, powerful roar of Das Boot's engine, and the next thing I knew, the wall across from me was hit with a huge, earthshaking crash that made the plaster pop, the window shatter and rain glass on me, and the wall bulge in. I peeped out from under my coat and saw a crack where smoke was rising, pouring out into the sky, grateful for release. I heard the roar of the engine, the squeal of wheels, and the whole building shook as my car rammed the wall violently once more. This time the stone and plaster broke, studs snapped, and then the crumpled, ash-strewn nose of my car was perched in the wall, opening like the mouth of a great white shark.

The driver's door opened, and then Bree was scrambling over rubble, coughing, and I reached out to her, and she grabbed my arms and hauled me out over the wreckage. Robbie was there outside, waiting for us, and as my knees buckled he ran over and caught me. I bent over, coughing and retching, while he and Bree held me.

Then we heard the nearing sounds of wailing fire sirens, and in the next few minutes three fire trucks appeared, Sky and Hunter arrived, and Cal's beautifully manicured lawn was ruined.

And I was alive.